REAWAKENING

A series of short stories between

The Hiding and The Somnia

Reawakening

A series of short stories between
The Hiding and The Somnia

by Alethea Lyons

Reawakening

All opinions expressed by characters in relation to magic and religion are their personal opinions and are subject to the rules of their universe, which are different from the rules of ours. No characters are scholars in this area, and all are simply coming from a place of trying to do good.

Edited by: S.D. Vassallo
Formatted by: Stephanie Ellis
Cover illustration and design by: Elizabeth Leggett

First Edition: September 2024
ISBN (paperback): 978-1-963355-05-5
ISBN (ebook): 978-1-963355-04-8
Library of Congress Control Number:

BRIGIDS GATE PRESS
Overland Park, Kansas
www.brigidsgatepress.com

Printed in the United States of America

To Marmee and Dad,
who gave me the gift of stories.

Content warnings are provided at the end of this book

CONTENTS

THE CLEANSING

A blood moon floats over York, bathing its ginnels and snickelways in rusty light. It hangs as a warning to those living below and a beacon for creatures lurking in the shadows. It can see what the humans of York cannot.

The moon sees the barghest, a black dog with eyes like fire. The barghest howls to the night and chains rattle against cobblestones in its wake. Behind it follows a motley crew of mongrels and purebreds alike. A funeral procession.

The moon sees a redcap flinging stones from the top of Clifford Tower. His hood is soaked in the blood of the many who have died there all the way back to William the Conqueror. In recent years, he has been contained, his power wan. His strength returns as the magic concealing it fades.

The moon sees Jenny Greenteeth, a river hag long banished from York, as she slips into the River Ouse. For many years she was forbidden to wade in its waters, but now no power exists to curb her penchant for dragging children to a dark demise.

As the moon watches, the mist spreads. Dark shadows unlimber. Long fingers cut through the air. Gaping maws announce the entrance to Hell. Vapours creep through alleyways and tumble down hills. Figures writhe in ghostly light, the moon's red tinge giving them the aspect of bloody corpses.

The mists are rising, and with them comes death.

The city lies in silence as the sun peeks its head over the horizon. The usual greetings to wake the city are conspicuously absent—the dual music of the cathedral bells and the muezzin reciting the adhan. Sounds of comfort and safety—silenced in the wake of tragedy.

Where the city walls cross the Ouse, four figures stand, two in the north of the city at each end of Lendal Bridge, two in the south at either side of Skeldergate Bridge. One wears a pointed mitre in gold and red and his glittering rosary catches the early sunlight. Another wears a plain cotton tunic and trousers, a stark contrast to the intricate prayer mat he kneels upon. The third wears ceremonial bana, her long hair concealed under a turban, the handle of a kirpan visible at her hip. The fourth wears a kippah on zir head and a tallit, a prayer shawl, across zir shoulders.

Along the banks of the river more people stand—a riot of colour representing dress and beliefs from across the globe. When the sun touches the river, each releases a floating candle onto its surface. The expanse of flames mirrors the glimmer of sunlight as it catches each ripple and peak.

As dawn bursts forth, the great bell of St. Peter's cathedral tolls. No carillon of joyous welcome to the sun. Slow. Measured. Funereal. The singing of the muezzin is melancholy in its beauty.

Tears glitter in the eyes of those along the riverbank, a microcosm of the shining surface that hides the true sorrow of the Ouse. In silence they retreat, allowing the twin melodies to warm their souls, praying it means peace will once again bless York.

Higher up the hill, watching from walled gardens and empty pub windows, another set of people stand. Their clothes are sombre, military. They clutch knives and guns. Sunlight glints off silver badges, cold where the candlelight diffusing over the river is soft. The image of a crown crossed by halberds was once a surety of safety, now an object of fear with so many citizens missing. Whether they were caught by the Queen's Guard or taken by the supernatural is unknown, so the people of York fear all in equal measure.

People flow past the Guard, giving them a wide berth without acknowledging their presence, each hoping to avoid notice. Even once the last of the faithful has left, the Queen's Guard stay, eyes fixed upon the river. To them, it is as if nothing has changed, as if the death of the river spirit means nothing. The Ouse still flows.

They do not notice the way the ducks squawk and flap as they dip their webbed feet into the water. They are unaware of the fish who slipped away during the night. They do not see the enticing green eyes and floating seaweed hair of Jenny Greenteeth as she awaits her first victim.

But others see and others know. York will never be the same again.

On Lendal Bridge, the Archbishop of York places his rosary back in its pouch and wipes his brow as his counterpart rolls up his prayer mat. They meet together at the apex of the bridge, staring down at the water below.

"Has your research yielded any results?" the archbishop asks in a low voice. His eyes flick to the top of Lendal Tower where a Guardsperson stands watch. The woman's eyes are fixed on the horizon yet he has no doubt she observes them.

The imam shakes his head. "Nothing. It is unclear whether the creature who was vanquished was a spirit possessing the river or an actual part of the river. We have no texts relating the origin of these types of creatures. We have observed changes in the animals and fish around the river. Even people have reported feelings of unease and fisherfolk are saying their nets are empty."

"The unease may be nothing more than a reaction to the murderous supernatural that lay hidden in the heart of the city. My archivists can find little more on the ritual the river spirit was trying to complete. We have told the Guard we have no knowledge of why these murders took place. The books which speak of it are forbidden texts; to reveal them would bring war between the Church and Guard."

"And by extension, the rest of the Council of Faiths." The imam lets out a long sigh. "It is a dangerous path you walk, old friend. If your people are indeed right and the spirit was attempting to complete a spell hiding others of her kind, then this could mean the end of York. Our night-safe status has already been revoked. The Queen's Guard hound our communities. If more supernaturals are to appear, war is upon us. The question remains, will the Guard be our ally or our enemy?"

"The enemy of my enemy is my friend, as they say." The archbishop glances up at the Guardswoman again. "Yet I suspect it would be a three-way battle. For now, I believe it's best for the Council to appear docile and choose our battles carefully. We shall continue to pursue information on those the Guard have disappeared. We have set our own task forces to watch for and deal with supernatural incursions. Thus far, there have been none. With last night being Hallowe'en and the final night of the ritual, we expected it, but the city was dead, if you'll excuse the expression."

"What of our new task force?" the imam asks. He waves a hand toward a group sitting on the banks of the river. Unlike most of the onlookers, they didn't move on when the prayers for the cleansing of the river finished. One young woman sits on the edge of the path, trailing her fingers through the water. The tip of her dark braid touches the surface. Next to her sits another woman. She pulls the first back from the water, a frown on her face. On the other side of them a young man crouches to fill test tubes with water then slots them into a storage box. He feels the imam's gaze and looks up to give the two religious leaders a friendly wave. The last of the group is lost in a world of his own, typing away on a laptop, barely noticing the rippling water or open sky.

The archbishop smiles fondly at the group. "If anyone can steer through these murky waters, it is my goddaughter and her foster sister. They don't know it, but their whole lives have been but a prelude to this. They will do what's right and what's needed."

"I have similar faith in Saqib," the imam agrees. "I don't know this other who has attached himself to them, though."

"He comes from an old Yorkshire family. I don't know them personally, but his mother is on the board of many of the charitable organisations in the city and surrounding area. From what Grace and Harper have told me, his technological expertise has been invaluable. It is a strange era we're living in, Mohammed. One where supernaturals must be fought online as well as with fire and swords. I'm glad to leave such things to younger folk."

The imam chuckles. "Quite right, Simon. We must have faith, in our people and in Allah who guides them."

The archbishop makes the sign of the cross over his chest. "We have much to do today. Let us leave the fight to them and go take care of our congregations."

The two men shake hands before each heads his separate way, the archbishop east towards the cathedral and the imam south towards the mosque.

Seen by neither, the mossy eyes of Jenny Greenteeth watch them go, submerged below the surface. The redcap lurks in dungeons buried deep underground, far from the sun's searing rays. The barghest sleeps in the shadows, no more than a normal hound. The brilliance of dawn has banished them. For now.

Until the moon rises again …

Never Alone Again

"Ms. De Santos, thank you for seeing us on such short notice." A prim lady in a floral hat peered up at Grace from the doorstep. A little girl of around six stood next to her, eyes downcast as she traced the edge of a paving slab with the toe of her patent leather shoe.

"Please come in, Mrs. Crawford, Meredith." Grace beckoned them down the hall to the lounge where Harper sat reading. "You remember my foster sister?"

"Of course." Mrs. Crawford gave Harper a polite nod which she returned.

"Can I get you anything? Tea, water, something to eat?" Grace offered but the woman shook her head.

"I'm sorry," she sniffed. "It's so upsetting that such a thing could happen to my little girl. I was almost on a train down to Canterbury to visit your father but he suggested I stop here first. He thought you might be able to help."

There was quiet desperation in the woman's voice but her daughter showed none of her agitation. Instead, the little girl sat with her hands folded neatly in her lap, her gaze never wavering from the intricate lace covering her knees.

Harper slipped out of the room and returned a minute later with a carafe of water. She poured a glass for the mother, who held it in her lap without drinking, her knuckles bone white around it. Harper half expected the glass to crack in her hands.

"We simply don't know what to do." A tear slid down Mrs. Crawford's cheek. Her pleading gaze never left Grace's face. "It's as if Meredith is possessed. Please, please tell me you can do something."

Harper handed a glass of water to the child who took it without a word, never lifting her eyes. She sipped her water but there was no sign of need or want, it was merely the next expected action.

"What makes you think so?" Grace asked.

Mrs. Crawford took her daughter's drink before replying. Water splashed onto the rug as the glass hit the table too hard and she clutched her shaking hands in her lap again.

"Meredith, dear, could you please write something for Ms. De Santos?" Mrs. Crawford asked.

"Of course, Mama." The childish voice was sweet and obedient. Nothing sounded amiss but still the girl did not look up.

Harper passed over the pad and pen Saqib kept by his chair to write down flashes of scientific inspiration. Meredith knelt on the floor at the coffee table, carefully arranging her layered skirts around her, the very picture of composure. "What should I write, Mama?"

Mrs. Crawford shuddered, her jaw tight as she replied, "Please write this week's Sunday school verse."

"Yes, Mama." The girl picked up the pen to write. Her head remained bowed, brown curls hiding her eyes. As she wrote, she muttered to herself.

"'*For God so loved the world, that he gave his only begotten Son, that whosoever believeth in him should not perish, but have everlasting life.*' Here, Mama." Without looking the girl slid the paper off the table and held it out to her waiting mother. Her movements were smooth, rehearsed, her voice flat.

Without speaking, Mrs. Crawford passed the sheet to Grace, who glanced at it then passed it to Harper. Reading it, Harper paled. The writing was spiked, as if the pen itself were enraged as it cut the words into the paper.

Ears Stone Deaf, Eyes Blind Shut. Fingers Broken, Heartstrings Cut.

Can't Hear Me, Can't See Me, Won't Hold Me, Don't Love Me.

Leave Me Alone & I'll KILL You.

Harper took a shaky breath then walked over to the hearth where she picked up a box of matches and lit one. She held the paper in the flame until it caught, then threw it in the fireplace. Once it was no more than ash, Harper turned and knelt next to the girl.

"May I?" she asked the mother, holding her hands over the child's head. Mrs. Crawford glanced at Grace, who nodded.

"I'm so sorry, I didn't know what else to do, I ..." Large gold rings clanked as Mrs. Crawford clenched her hands in her lap.

"There is no need to apologise." Grace rested a hand on their visitor's arm. "You did the right thing. My father taught us how to deal with such things."

"But what is it?" Mrs. Crawford wailed. "Is she bewitched? Cursed? *Possessed?*"

"Perhaps you should wait in the kitchen." Grace helped the older woman to her feet and steered her out of the room.

Harper placed a hand on the girl's forehead. Despite the warmth of the day, her skin was cold and clammy. Letting her hair fall over her face, concealing her violet gaze, Harper watched the child through her Sight. The burning sensation of magic came swiftly as though the child's desperation to be perceived dragged it out of her.

"Look at me." Harper lifted the girl's chin.

The child's eyes met Harper's Sight.

With a yelp, Harper fell back, bashing her elbow against the coffee table. The hairs on the back of her neck prickled when she raised her head to meet the girl's gaze again. A chill ran down her spine, oozed between her vertebrae, and dribbled over her ribs until the cold all but stopped her breath. Faint wisps hung in the air before her, the fire's heat more distant than the sun. She swallowed the bile in her throat and blinked, eyelids rasping over her cornea. Meredith blinked back at her, black membrane shuttering her eyes horizontally. Large pupils dominated, wreathed by vermillion irises.

"*You See me.*" The multi-tonal voice contained both the high-pitch of the child and the deeper, gravelly tones of something darker and older.

"What are you?" Harper whispered.

The child's lips twitched into a contorted smile. "*I am a friend.*"

"Whose friend?" Harper asked, unable to tear herself away from the hollow eyes of the girl. Meredith's pupils widened, a black hole that sucked all light from the room. The fire diminished to sparks and cinder. Frost clawed at the windows.

"*Why, Meredith's of course. She was so lonely. So tired of being good.*" The girl's laugh rattled like jagged glass.

"Why her?" Harper's mouth moved but the words came from a great distance.

"*She wished it.*" The girl tilted her head to the side, pink lips twitched to a knife-edge smile. Harper's lips stretched, aching. "*What do* you *wish, Seer? You have the Power.*"

"Does *she* have the Power?" The words hung between them, almost visible in the vaporous air.

When the child spoke, Harper's lips moved with her, a silent echo. "*Meredith was lonely. She found me. I wrote her plea to her mother, her father, her teacher, her priest. None of them listened. You are the first to See me.*"

Pressure built behind Harper's eyes as though someone had thrust their fingers into her skull and tried to force them out of their sockets. She wanted to blink, to shut her eyes tight before they burst. Meredith's eyes widened, pinning Harper's lids open, reflecting her violet stare.

"'Children should be seen, not heard.' That's what they always tell her. Her cries fell on uncaring ears so I wrote her pain for all to see. I am her friend. Her protector." The girl tilted her head, curls bouncing on her shoulders. Harper's head snapped to the side. *"Now you have Seen. What will you do?"*

"She doesn't have to be alone anymore." Harper managed to force the words through cracked lips. "We'll make sure she's taken care of. I'll be her friend. I promise." Her constricting throat choked on the words. Pain seared her lungs and heart as the oath took hold.

"Then Meredith's wish is answered. What is your wish, Seer? I can see that which is hidden within you, the twisted path to the past. Will you let me help you?"

"I …" Crimson eyes bored into hers, consuming her will. The little girl tilted her head the other way and Harper's head jerked, a perfect reflection.

"All you need do is wish it and I am yours." The voice lowered, losing the childish quality, becoming seductive, beguiling. The girl leant forward and the invisible bond drew Harper toward her. Their foreheads almost touched. The little girl raised her hand, one finger curled in beckoning. Bone ground against bone as Harper's hand rose and contorted in a mirrored claw.

"Let me be with you." Darkness consumed the girl's eyes and the void sucked Harper in deeper. *"Let me love you."*

Harper's lips mirrored the words. "Love … you …"

"What do you wish, Seer?" So close their mouths were almost touching, the words exhaled on Meredith's breath were sucked through Harper's lips and became part of her. *"Wish for your heart's desire."*

"I wish …"

"Harper!"

Sharp heat gouging her arm forced Harper's watering eyes closed and the spell was broken. It took great effort for her to turn and stare wide-eyed at Grace who was sitting next to her holding a smoking match.

"I'm sorry, I couldn't snap you out of it." Grace tossed the match into the fireplace.

Harper shook her head. Frissons of pain lanced down her aching spine. "No, I needed it."

The little girl sat with her head bowed once more but her voice still contained a shadow of darkness.

"You refuse my gift. Beware, Seer, you denounce more than just my help. You denounce your own past, forever to dwell in mists and shadows. Farewell, Meredith. I loved you."

The girl looked up and for a moment her eyes glowed ruby red, then the colour faded to pink before it vanished into the whirlpool of her dilated pupils, which diminished to mere pinpricks. With a soft sigh, Meredith's blue eyes rolled back in her head and she collapsed.

Grace caught her before her head hit the floor. She cradled the unconscious child in her arms. "Do you think it's gone?"

"Yes? I mean, yes." The shadows had receded, the air clear again, but Harper could feel the darkness clinging to her. She pulled her knees up to her chest, wrapping her arms around them as she tried to sound more confident. "Definitely. It came because she wished for a friend. Once she found one, it had no more hold over her. I'm not sure where it went."

"Her mother said it started after her sister died." Grace brushed aside brown ringlets to check the child's pulse. "She'll be okay. Just needed some love, poor thing. Her mother said they would hear her talking but when they entered the room no one else was there. 'Children should be seen and not heard,' huh? My guess is she made an imaginary friend to replace her sister and, when that outlet was banned, the spirit replaced the imaginary friend. Until she finds some friends her own age, she'll have us." Grace reached over and squeezed Harper's arm. "And we'll make sure her parents know to be a little more lenient."

Later, once Mrs. Crawford and Meredith had left, Grace and Harper sat in the kitchen, a pot of tea on the table between them. Each clutched her mug with both hands but neither made a move to drink.

"Do you think she meant what she wrote?" Harper asked, breaking the heavy silence. "I get that telling her mother she was possessed is a bad idea. Telling her it was grief and a plea for attention, that she needs counselling, is even true in a way. But … if the spirit was only giving her what she wished for …"

"She's six," Grace said. "I don't think she had any idea what she was writing. I think she meant to write her Sunday school verse. If we don't believe that then …"

"Then there is more trouble there than we can help with," Harper finished with a shudder.

"Time will tell," Grace said, finally taking a sip of her tea. "At least she's getting help."

"I think it did care for her." Harper stared into the murky brown depths of her mug. "It may have simply been its own wish to be adored but it did care."

"A sister can never be replaced," Grace said firmly.

Harper lifted her cup to her lips. It was a strain to move. The hot tea seeped between her lips, coated her tongue, and trickled down her throat. It washed away some of her lethargy.

"Hey, Harp. Is there something *you* want to talk about?"

"Like what?" Harper looked up, head tilted, eyes wide.

Grace pressed her lips together as she stared at her sister. "The demon's offer. You were tempted. If something's wrong, I wish you'd tell me."

Harper frowned for a moment then let out a deep breath. She stood and walked around the table to sit next to Grace. Wrapping her arms around her sister, Harper snuggled up and lay her head against Grace's shoulder. "Nothing's wrong, but I guess I *was* tempted. It might've known the way home."

Grace rested her head against Harper's, stroking her hair. "I promise, Harp, one day you and I will find your kin."

"I know." Harper twisted her fingers into her sister's top, the burning in her eyes nothing to do with magic.

"Harp?"

Harper sat up to meet Grace's clear, brown eyes.

"You will always, *always* have a home with me," Grace promised. "Always."

What's Eating the Cows?

Harper's new sneakers were covered in urine-coloured mud, her jeans were beyond saving, and she didn't want to think about how many bottles of shampoo would be needed for her hair. If this wasn't resolved quickly, someone was going to regret it. Her face twisted in a grim smile. Viscous blood slithered down her blade and hissed onto the floor.

The creature smirked, lips drawn back to reveal two rows of serrated, crimson teeth with strips of flesh dangling between them. A cackle bubbled from its throat as it shook its putrid green mane. Droplets of blood flew off to splatter against the barn walls.

Russet fur stood on end as it growled and its massive paws scratched straw soaked in dung and blood. Six spindly arms protruded from its jointed, insectoid torso. Fingers, barely more than jagged nails, clicked together in irritation.

It leapt at Harper. Spear-like claws sliced through the air. She parried two long arms at once as it tried to eviscerate her. The tiger-like front paws swiped at her as she dived out the way. They caught her side, knocked the air out of her. She hit the ground hard. Pain lanced through her back as her tailbone cracked against stone. With a lightness belied by its mismatched limbs, the creature spun. Harper rolled to the side, her blind swing skittering off the creature's armoured carapace as her attacker pounced where she'd lain a moment before. Something soft and malodorous squished beneath her and Harper winced, trying not to think about it as she dragged herself to her feet.

"Anytime, Grace," Harper muttered. "What the hell's taking her so long?" Harper backed away from the creature, circling it slowly. Its tail slashed a warning and she parried with her blade. Her sharp weapon caught the stinger and scored deep into the thin tail. The creature howled as the tip of its tail fell twitching to the ground. It thrashed the severed stump, blood slapping the wall like cast-off from a knife, splattering across Harper's jeans and shoes.

I liked these sneakers, they're comfy. Harper didn't have time for regret as the creature sprang. She raised her blade as the heavy body crashed into her but the tearing of claw and nail never came. Harper rolled as she fell, avoiding getting stuck under the monster, rising to a defensive crouch.

The creature lay before her, moaning in a disconcertingly human tone. A thick bolt protruded from its chest. It shuddered, then lay still, mewling softly.

"Finally." Harper glared into the shadows behind her. "It took you long enough."

"Sorry, Harp. Didn't see your message. You okay?" Grace emerged, notching another bolt into the groove of a handheld crossbow. Her outfit was pristine, her black stiletto heels shining. She walked with a swish in her hips. The only small thing out of place was the slight smudge in her red lipstick.

"*Okay?* Do I look okay, Gray? I left you five voicemails and seven texts. I couldn't wait any longer. Where were you?"

Grace shrugged and her usual swagger slipped away. Her nose wrinkled as she surveyed her foster sister's bedraggled form. "I … uh … Well, you needed the practice and I knew you could handle this and—"

"And you had a date," Harper finished, arms folded across her chest. "Why can't you answer your bloody phone?"

"Why are you out hunting?" Grace threw back at her.

"Gray …" Harper trailed off, tugging at her braid on autopilot. Her face twisted in a grimace as she yanked her hand away from its stomach-turning slickness. She shook the grime off her hand then rubbed it almost clean on her last patch of unsoiled clothing.

"I know. We're responsible, now." Grace lifted her hand to pat Harper's shoulder then thought better of it. "What is this thing, anyway? How did you find out about it?"

"Bit of scrying. I was looking for Melissa Heyes, she's on the archbishop's missing people list. Guess magic has a bad sense of humour, or Heresy's messing with me again." Harper lifted a piece of hay off the ground, twirling it between her fingers. "Couldn't find Mel. Did find half a dozen eviscerated cows. Don't go in the next barn over if you ever want to eat beef again, that's all I'm saying. What are we doing to do with it?"

Grace surveyed the moaning creature with cold eyes as she aimed her crossbow again. "What we do with all rabid animals. Put it down." There was a loud crack and the moaning ceased.

Harper raised an eyebrow as she looked across at her sister. "That was a bit cold for a vet, wasn't it?"

Grace shrugged a shoulder. "Maybe, but I can hardly take this thing back in a kitty cage, can I? Anyway, it sounded good. If we're going to build a reputation of our own, not just the De Santos Family rep, we gotta sound good." She looked Harper up and down out of the corner of her eye and added under her breath, "And look good."

"There's no one here." Harper threw up her hands in aggravation then winced as blood flew off her blade and splattered across Grace's jeans. Grace's eyes narrowed. "Let's chalk it up as experience and go home."

"Those are only tranq-bolts," Grace informed her. "That new formula Saqib was working on was effective. He'll be happy, at least."

Harper tucked her machete safely behind her back. *Never put a blade away dirty.* She could hear Grace's oldest brother's voice in her mind, scolding, but there was nothing to clean it on.

"What do you want to do with it?" Grace gestured towards the unconscious creature.

Harper paused. It probably weighed more than both women put together and she didn't relish the idea of butchering it and moving it piecemeal.

"Take photos then banish it before it heals?" she suggested. "That is, if you remembered to bring your phone with you."

With a scornful eye-roll, Grace took her phone out of her pocket and snapped a few pictures so they could research what the creature was later. Heresy would probably know, or AJ could look it up online. If neither of them could find it, then Harper could sneak the photos into the cathedral archives and see what was in the Vault.

While Grace recorded the bizarre animal, Harper pushed aside the hay and other bovine detritus to make a relatively clear space on the barn floor. She drew a large, slightly lopsided, circle by pouring a thin stream of salt from the bag and marked off the cardinal points. At each, she sketched a quick picture of one of the core elements. Grace raised an eyebrow at the unsightly 'supermarket's cheapest' bag the salt was in, but didn't mention anything about 'looking good' again.

Once ready, the two women hefted the creature into the circle Harper had made. Grace stepped back, her lip curled in disgust as Harper walked widdershins about the circle. She muttered a spell, hand extended over the slumbering whatever-it-was. Heresy recommended she use an object to focus. Fear of being detained and having to explain a wand or athame to the police or Guard stopped Harper from following his instruction. That and it felt silly and unnatural to her.

Remembering Heresy's teachings, she pictured energy coming up through the earth, through her poor, unsavable sneakers, to flow through her body. To Harper, it was as though the salt caught fire, glowing a brilliant violet against the brown-and-grey floor. "The time of sending is here, go to a place none will fear. Never to come here again, spirits rid us of this bane."

The searing flash burned her retinas, even through her eyelids. Air rushed from her lungs as though dragged away by the banishing. When the light faded, the creature was gone. Harper doubled over, hands clasping her knees as she fought to stay upright. Her sister hovered close by, hand outstretched to help, nose wrinkled. Harper waved her away, rubbing her forehead as she righted herself. Her eyelids dragged like she hadn't slept for a week. She'd been doing too much magic recently, and too much fighting. Everything ached.

"You're getting good at that," Grace observed as Harper scuffed out the circle.

"Heresy doesn't think so. He says it's sloppy magic and I should use crystals and wands and all sorts. He said it makes the magic neater, less likely to spill out and attract attention, and that it makes it easier on me."

"You get caught with crystals in your purse and you're as good as dead."

"I know. I'm not entirely sure he's telling the truth, about that or the spell words he gives me. He might find it funny. I wish I knew where it went to. Heresy said it's okay but these circles could send things to someone's bedroom for all I know."

"It would've been on the news." Grace gave a dismissive wave of her hand.

"I don't know." Harper tugged her braid on autopilot and winced again. "Look at all the stuff that happens and *isn't* reported. Most of the creatures we've fought are pretty mindless but something out there is covering tracks. This isn't the first incursion since the Ouse's death. If someone isn't covering it up, someone other than us, then it would have been front page news."

"A problem for another day," Grace said pragmatically. "For now, let's go shower and change."

"Yeah." Harper grimaced again. She wished she could block out the smell. "We've saved the farm and I think a shower is a brilliant reward. Let's go home."

"When's the next bus?" Grace asked as they headed back towards the main road.

Harper checked her watch. She smeared grime around its face as she tried to read it. "Forty-five minutes."

"Geez, my shoes are squelching. Can we take a cab?"

"No way they let us in a cab."

"No way they let us on a bus."

The two exchanged a glance, a mirrored smile cracking.

"Saqib!" they said in chorus.

"Thank heavens we have a friend with a car," Harper added.

"Might not be our friend for long," Grace pointed out. "You could let me get a car."

"The police won't let you drive, you maniac."

"It was one red light."

"It was not."

Their voices faded into the darkness.

The Pūca in the Priory

Chanting twisted through moist air, ethereal as the moaning of a ghost. Notes ricocheted off headstones, echoing in minor keys. Dense fog muffled and distorted the sound with its own dissonance. Barely visible through silvery mist, a grey stone church loomed against the backdrop of a rain-laden sky.

The wrought iron gate squealed as Harper placed a hand on it, barely moving it. She sucked in cold air, then shoved the gate fast. Its scream ripped through the night. A banshee's wail.

Then silence.

The chant had stopped.

Harper and Grace paused inside the gate. Harper's machete was already in her hand, knuckles white around its grip. Grace slid a bolt into the groove of her handheld crossbow. The tight lines around her eyes mirrored the taut string of the weapon. Catching Harper's eye, she nodded towards the western door, then pointed to herself and gestured towards the south transept entrance. Harper returned her nod before stepping off the path onto dew-soaked grass.

Tombstone slabs lay side by side like ancient standing stones long since fallen and forgotten. On each a name, a date of birth, a date of death. The edges of the lettering glimmered with purple fire, the burning in Harper's eyes a giveaway that she was Seeing some magic at work.

"Leave them alone." She scuffed at the flames with her shoe. Vapours poured into the gaps and swirled about her feet.

A low chuckle drifted through the mists and a black shadow solidified at her feet.

"Heresy?"

A black cat rubbed its head against her ankle. Its rumbling purr travelled up her leg like a nervous twitch.

"Harper, dearest, do you speak to the dead now?" The voice emanating from the cat was amused, mocking. "Do you expect them to answer?"

Harper glanced southwards, but Grace was lost in the thickening fog.

"I don't have time for this." She pushed Heresy away with her foot. "We'll work out why the tombstones are bespelled later."

Heresy chuckled, cat-tongue flicking between teeth bared in a mischievous leer. "Because humans are odd creatures. Why do they leave flowers, candles, and toys for those who have gone to the great beyond? In this day and age, most do not believe the deceased can take such baubles with them, so why do they bother?"

"Do you mean this is human magic? Cast by witches? Like me?" Despite the gloom around them, Harper couldn't keep the squeak of excitement out of her voice.

"For once, you are surprisingly astute." Heresy chuckled.

"Can we watch this place and meet them?" Harper knelt to brush her fingers over a muddy name. Lilac flames licked at her skin, colder than mist or stone. She snatched her hand back, sucking her fingers until they could feel her tongue.

Heresy huffed a sigh. "A return to normal. Can you not tell the age of this magic. Those who left this tribute are long since departed and lying under stone themselves."

"That doesn't mean their descendants aren't around. AJ can do some kind of family tree thing based on the gravestones, or—" The silence was shattered by a crash from within the priory. Someone screamed and Harper jumped to her feet. Monks were yelling. The stench of smoke filled the air.

Harper dashed to the door, yanked it open, weapon held out steady in front of her.

Chaos greeted her.

Monks scrambled to put out fires, grabbing melting wax in bare hands to yank flames away from hymnals and prayer books. Hanging crooked on the stone walls were colourful banners depicting the stations of the cross. One was ripped in two, ragged ends fluttering. Another lay trampled on the ground, the edges smouldering. Tongues of fire licked up the altar cloth from a fallen candle at its base. Flames coughed up charcoal-grey smoke that hung heavy below wooden ceiling beams. Smoke mingled with incense, harmonious scents, bitter and funereal.

Wooden pews were overturned, angled like barricades, tonsured heads bowed behind them. Harper ducked down next to one of them who didn't even notice the intrusion. She could just make out Grace's dark locks peeking out behind a pillar at the other end of the church.

One man stood in the centre of the priory nave, a crucifix held out in front of him like a shield. His arm trembled and he leant back poised to flee. Harper couldn't make out his frenzied mumbling, just the movement of his lips repeating something over and over. At the edge of the north and south transepts, two other monks stood similarly, one holding a Bible in front of him and the other clutching his rosary.

Their fevered prayers had no effect whatsoever on the bizarre creature crouching in between them where the two arms of the church crossed. Harper peered around the edge of the makeshift barrier to watch it. It wasn't quite an animal she was familiar with, but close, as though drawn by a child. A scruff of long hair ran from its head all the way down its back to a tail tufted like a lion's. It stood on four legs and its fur was a slightly mottled, but bright, orange. A long nose gave a dog-like cast to its face, yet the curve of its mouth and the shape of its eyes were so human, tears came to Harper's eyes at its expression of abject misery.

If it was aware of the chaos around it, the creature gave no indication. It didn't even look at the monks who were attempting to banish it. Instead, it stared intently at a large tome on the floor. With a flick of its paw, it flipped through the pages, each touch surprisingly delicate. Harper wondered how much of the damage around her had been done by this confused visitor and how much was a result of the monks' own panic.

Harper darted closer, ducking in and out of cover, to get an angle where she could see the book. The creature stopped on a page showing a light-grey-and-blue animal with knobbly knees and cloven hooves. Harper squinted. It almost looked like a camel. With its head tipped to one side, the creature leant over to study the picture with its nose almost touching the page. Then it changed.

Toes fused then cracked into hooves. Legs elongated with a stomach-turning pop. Its neck stretched as though a noose dragged it while its belly distended and bloated. Lumps rose under the skin of its back, bursting out like pustules.

The monk in front of Harper dropped his crucifix with a strangled yell. Scattered books and broken wood tripped his scrambling retreat. He looked at Harper in wide-eyed terror when she caught his shoulder yet he offered no resistance as she tucked him behind a pew with his fellows. Silence returned as she stepped forward, all eyes riveted on her. Out the corner of her eye, Grace sharply gestured no. As Harper approached, a black cat trotted up beside the creature and rubbed its nose against the ungulate's leg.

"Hello. I'm Harper. I can help you." As Harper approached the creature, she held a hand out like she was greeting a stray cat or dog. She stopped next to the book and held her upturned palm under the creature's nose. It gave her a cursory sniff. For a moment, Harper feared it was working on a globule of spit to fire at her, but when its mouth opened it was words, not saliva, that emerged.

"Hello, Lady Harper. How may I help you?" The voice was thick, unsurprising given the awkward shape of the creature's mouth and throat. The words were uncertain, learnt by rote but not really understood.

"I'm here to help you." When the creature didn't object, Harper placed her hand on its neck, stroking until zir trembling ceased. "I don't think you meant to come here, did you?"

"I wanted to read the book."

Flesh writhed and shifted under Harper's hand. She snatched it back, clenching her teeth to hold back bile as the creature transformed. Ze shrank rapidly, bones cracking, skin saggy then snapping into place. The creature's face squished in as though punched, whiskers popped from zir cheeks, and zir tail stretched like elastic. In a matter of moments, two black cats sat staring at each other. Heresy lifted a paw and the shapeshifter mirrored him.

Harper sat cross-legged on the cold, stone floor, picked up the open book, and patted her knee. The creature slunk over and climbed into her lap like a child ready for story time. With a dainty paw, ze flipped the pages until ze reached an illustration labelled 'Cat and Mouse.' Ze looked at the blue-and-white-striped cat with its long neck and broad shoulders, then looked at the cat whose body Heresy was possessing.

"This bestiary is very old," Harper explained. "I know someone who has some real animals you can imitate, if you'll let me take you to him."

The shapeshifter nodded. "That would be fun, Lady Harper."

Trying not to smile at the shock on the monks' faces, Harper cuddled the cat inside her jacket. As she stepped towards the open transept door, one of the monks blocked her path. He thrust his Bible in her face, almost smacking her on the nose with it. "Begone foul witch and take your demon familiar with you."

Harper's breath caught in her throat. Her chest heaved with the exertion of drawing in oxygen as a weight crashed down on her. Tears gathered in her eyes, leaving no moisture in her mouth as her lips formed a hollow denial.

Her eyes. They weren't burning. But they must be violet. How else could he know?

"Don't be ridiculous." A well-manicured hand batted the Bible out of Harper's face. Grace took up a protective stance next to her, crossbow bolt notched. "My sister is *not* the threat here." Grace waved a slip of paper bearing an impression of crossed keys in crimson wax. "We have been sent by my godfather, the Archbishop of York, to save your sorry asses and your ramshackle church. Would you rather she confronted the demon head on and burned down what little you have left? How many generations has *your* family been hunting demons? None? Then leave extraction and disposal to the experts."

Grace grabbed Harper's arm then shouldered the monk aside as she dragged her sister out of the church. The cat in Harper's arms trembled and snuggled in closer against her. Heresy followed them out with his nose and tail in the air, the triumphant ending of a less than victorious parade.

"You aren't helping," Harper informed him when they were far enough away from the church for the fog to mask sight and sound of them.

Heresy grinned up at her. "That depends upon whom you think my help is being bestowed."

Rolling her eyes, Grace knelt, scooped up Heresy, and gave him a shake. "You get out of that poor cat at once. You hear me? If anyone is going to be banishing a demon this evening, you better believe it'll be *me* banishing *you*."

Puffs of smoke rose from bristled fur as the cat tensed in Grace's hands, claws extended. It swiped at her and she dropped it. As its feet hit the pavement, it was already running, a black blur against grey fog. Heresy floated down onto Harper's shoulder, once again nothing more than a ball of static and soot.

"You spoil all my fun, Grace," he chuckled.

"What are you going to do with that?" Grace ignored Heresy to prod the animal tucked inside Harper's jacket.

Harper pushed her hand away. "Do you have a name?" she asked the creature.

"What name do you like?"

"I like … James."

"That's funny. My name is James."

Harper laughed. "It's nice to meet you, James. Do you have any pronouns?"

The creature shook zir head. "I can be either gender."

"So we can help you get home, what are you and where do you come from?"

"I'm a pūca. I come from …" The pūca wrinkled its nose. "I don't know. But I saw the book with all the animals in it and it looked fun."

"I think ze's just a baby," Harper whispered to Grace as the pūca examined zir paws. "AJ said there's a guy who might be able to help if we didn't want to kill or banish whatever we found. Said this 'zookeeper' fellow keeps some kind of magical menagerie, but he'll help out sentients as well. Maybe he's seen one of these before."

Grace watched the creature with narrow eyes, then her brow unfurrowed and she stretched out a finger to stroke its head. "I think you're right. We'll tell godfather we took ze far away from Mickelgate Priory and disposed of ze safely. It'll even be true."

"In the future, maybe the monks will be a bit more careful about leaving ancient manuscripts lying around." Harper sniffed, the archivist in her bristling at the casual treatment of such an old text. "Really, that book should be behind glass. Poor James. Ze never stood a chance of blending in. The thirteenth century monks who drew it had no clue what any of those animals really looked like, although you'd think they'd've seen a cat before."

Grace groaned. "Am I in for another lecture on the inaccuracy of historical texts?"

"Well, is it any wonder it's difficult to discern true folklore from superstition when the recordkeepers of seven centuries ago couldn't even draw a cat?" As they talked, they headed back toward the city centre and home. Harper cuddled the pūca against her chest to keep it safe from the grasp of the chilling mist. "Someone probably saw that illustration and thought there was a cat sidhe lurking. It also throws into doubt the accuracy of any actual supernatural creatures they encountered."

"What does a pūca look like in its natural form?" Grace asked, curious despite herself.

"That is a very rude question," Heresy huffed. "You would not like it if I asked for details about your natural form."

"That's entirely different." Grace walked faster, her nose in the air, but she didn't repeat the question.

When they got home, they made the pūca a bed from a cardboard box and an old blanket. James seemed content to stay cat-shaped, so Harper figured it was easiest to treat zir as such. She fed zir some cat food left over from the last time Grace had brought a stray home from the clinic. It had been a short-lived visit thanks to Heresy's meddling and there were several tins of food remaining.

The next morning, a grumpy Saqib was dragged out of bed early and drove Harper and James to the Zookeeper's before work. They were greeted there by an almost human-looking woman in overalls, who took James and made a big fuss over zir. Her reptilian eyes regarded him with genuine delight.

"We'll take good care of zir and find zir a new home, never you fear," the woman assured Harper. "There'll be more like zir in days to come. Folk are flocking here and not all of them should be allowed to roam free."

Going Around in Circles

"There's no evidence whatsoever. It's brilliant."

Harper raised an eyebrow at Saqib's enthusiasm. "Excuse the ignorance of a non-scientist, but isn't zero evidence bad?"

"Very." Saqib's grin widened for a moment before his expression sobered. "We've tracked five missing people to this park in the last week. Nothing connects them, they're all different ages, races, social backgrounds. There's no CCTV in the park itself, but there's fairly comprehensive coverage around the perimeter. They go in. They don't come out. They just vanish. There's no sign of a struggle or recently disturbed dirt. I even looked up in the trees in case it was something flying or vampiric or whatever."

Harper smiled at the mental image of the laidback Saqib excitedly climbing half the trees in the park. No wonder he was unusually dishevelled, his curly hair messy and his clothes streaked with drying mud. From where they stood at the south entrance, the park looked like any other in the watery morning sunlight. Ice glittered on the tip of each blade of grass giving an illusion of scattered crystals. Light mist curled around the base of trees. Jagged silhouettes of branches fractured a cloudless blue sky and framed children playing football between clothes-pile goals while parents wandered down the paths, chatting and drinking takeaway coffee.

As they headed further in, Saqib continued, "Each morning it's as if no one has been in the park for a hundred years. There are no footprints, no broken grass or flowers, no cigarette butts or other litter. Whoever is taking people isn't just tidying up after themselves, they're tiding up the whole park. What human killer would bother with that?"

If someone had meticulously cleaned the park the night before, then someone else had trashed it again since. Harper picked up a crisp packet and stuffed it into a nearly empty bin just as a jogger trotted past and threw an empty bottle of water on the ground.

"Hey—" she protested but they were already gone.

They wandered around the park at a casual pace, trying to blend in. Heresy had accompanied Harper and he flitted from dog to dog, keeping his eyes and noses open and the grumbling to a minimum. He really preferred cats.

They were strolling across a wide, grassy area when Harper grabbed Saqib's arm and yanked him back.

"Dog poop," she said loudly as she dragged him away.

"What is it?" Saqib asked quietly. Sitting down on a nearby bench, Harper pointed.

"Faery circle. See?"

Saqib squinted. "Are you sure?"

"Certain. It makes sense too. Faeries look after nature and there's lots of stories of them taking revenge on those who harm it and lots of stories about people who went into faery circles and vanished. It explains why the park has less evidence after the crime. If the park is always as messy as it is today, I understand why they're angry. On the positive side it means the missing people probably aren't dead. On the negative side; they could be very difficult to get back. Honestly, I'm not really comfortable with destroying the circle. Humans are the ones messing up the park. All the faeries want to do is tidy up."

"It doesn't excuse kidnapping." There was an anger in Saqib's voice Harper had never heard before. She placed a hand on his shoulder and was surprised to find him shaking.

"Of course it doesn't. But maybe there's a better way to solve this than by destroying something. Maybe if they don't think we're a threat, the faeries will give our people back."

"Assuming they're still alive to come back. It's been well-documented that people who step into fae dimensions can reappear five minutes later after having lived their whole lives there. Or can reappear after a hundred years looking exactly as they did the day they left." Saqib stared at the circle, his eyes unfocused.

"You okay?" Harper squeezed his shoulder when he didn't respond.

He shook himself. "Yeah, sorry. Just …" He took a deep breath. "My grandmother disappeared like that."

"I'm so sorry." Harper hugged his shoulders. "What happened? Did she come back?"

Saqib hung his head, turning his face away. "It was before I was born. Mum was a baby, but some of my older aunts and uncles remember it. They said their mother walked into a circle of trees and never came out the other side. It was hushed up so the Queen's Guard wouldn't get involved.

It's one of the reasons I research supernatural forensics. I always hoped one day I'd find a way to bring her back."

"You will," Harper said. "We will. Whether it's your science or my … abilities, or both. We'll find a way to bring them back."

"Thanks, Harp." Saqib sniffed, then wiped his eyes on the back of his sleeve. "If we can get these people back, then maybe there's hope."

"Woof."

A spaniel ran up to them, tail wagging, and Harper patted it on the head. "You're not supposed to say 'woof,' but since you're here can you run the perimeter of a faery circle for me?"

"Woof."

The dog ran off to sniff the ground around the circle despite the calls of its exasperated owners. Harper rolled her eyes. Heresy was perfectly capable of communicating in English while inhabiting an animal, he was being ornery because she told him off the week before for being too conspicuous. After running a couple of rings, the dog ran back to its owner and a black shadow slid out of it, across the ground, and came to rest against Harper's shoe.

"It is a big one," Heresy whispered. "Stinks of pesky faeries. I can eat them?" For a moment the shadow split revealing sharp, white teeth.

"You may not," Harper reprimanded as Saqib snorted in laughter.

"It would solve your problem and I am hungry," Heresy complained.

"It wouldn't solve my problem in the slightest. We need to talk to them."

"Because that went well last time," Saqib said. "If you try to talk to them then I hypothesise that the next missing person will be you, Harper."

"Maybe Grace?" Harper suggested.

"Grace is a hothead. She'd be even worse."

"But she's a hothead about the same stuff that's bothering the faeries," Harper explained. "They might respect a vet."

"Faeries respect nothing," Heresy grumped.

"They respect this park. I would be mad if I cleaned my home each night and then every morning someone came and trashed it."

Saqib coughed. It sounded remarkably like, 'AJ.'

"Your cereal bowl from this morning is clean and in the cupboard is it?" Harper gave him a pointed look. Saqib examined a whisp of cloud drifting overhead and whistled nonchalantly.

"We'll come back nearer sundown. Saqib, you can set up your equipment then. Nothing invasive. Monitoring only. If you can find a way to detect them, then great, but don't risk Grace. At midnight we'll see what happens. At the very least we can stop people walking into the circle."

"I can pop some police tape around it to keep people out. I'm going to hang around and do some calibrations. Is it dangerous?"

"I don't think so as long as you stay out of the circle and don't drop any litter or damage any plants."

"Meet back here at twenty-three forty-five?"

"Sure, I'll brief Grace."

The vet clinic was heaving. Harper cautiously skirted a pile of drool, which may have been a dog in another life, and a particularly evil-looking feline.

"Ooh, fun." The warm presence around her neck disappeared as Heresy left her to possess the cat. Harper ignored him and continued through the live obstacle course until she reached the reception desk. "Hey, Julia."

"Hi Harper." The receptionist gave her a strained smile. "If you're here for Grace, you've got a wait. We're a little busy and she's currently in surgery."

"I'll leave a message," Harper said. "Can you ask her to call me when she has a sec? Before eleven tonight, the earlier the better. It's a family thing."

"You guys have one weird family, ya know? I'll pass on the message."

"Thanks, Julia. Good luck."

Harper picked her way back out of the clinic. At least with Julia, she could be sure Grace would get the message. Her sister had the bad habit of ignoring voicemails. Electronic communication made Harper uncomfortable anyway, although AJ had put some sort of electronic hex on their phones which should mask anything they didn't want the Queen's Guard to detect if they were snooping.

In an effort to overcome her own silly superstition, Harper pulled out her mobile and dialled.

"Hey, AJ. Have you eaten yet? … Of course not … Wanna grab some dinner? The others won't be home … Yeah, I can bring takeout. You pick the film."

Grace's call had been brief and to the point but she showed up at the park, only a few minutes late, and stalked past Harper and Saqib without a word.

"Who spat in her tea?" Saqib asked as Grace brushed off his greeting.

"Me, I think." Harper grimaced. "She's mad at me for disturbing her at work."

"So, what am I doing?" Grace stood at the edge of the faery circle, arms crossed, foot tapping. As Harper explained, Grace's expression softened slightly. "Okay then. I guess you had a good reason, but next time you come to my work, leave the blasphemous cloud at home."

Harper tugged her braid. In her hurry to get out of the clinic, she'd forgotten to pick up Heresy. It was just like him to have made his presence known to Grace rather than lying low or making his own way back.

"I'm sorry, Grace, I was in a rush. I shouldn't have brought him in with me."

Grace gave a short nod. "We've got a job to do. You folks better back off to a safe distance. If this goes badly, you come get me, got it?"

"Of course." Harper joined Saqib over by the bench. In her absence, he had set up a variety of strange-looking equipment and was currently fiddling with a handheld remote control.

"Ready?" Harper asked him.

"Nearly." He frowned at his apparatus. "I need to recalibrate a bit. Grace is interfering."

As Saqib wandered off muttering to himself, Harper took a seat and waited.

Great Peter's midnight toll rolled over the city. In the wake of the bell, a strange stillness spread through the park, as if the minute of midnight lingered past its allotted time. The starless, moonless sky offered no light. Long, twisting shadows cracked grass yellowed by the distant streetlamps. Mists clung to the stony paths, roiling where they met grass or trees and the bins resembled witches' cauldrons as the vapours oozed over them.

A slight giggle and a brief flash of movement out of the corner of her eye alerted Harper to the faeries' presence but she kept her gaze locked on Grace. The other woman knelt at the edge of the circle. Harper could just make out the movement of her lips and the crease of her brow. If she squinted, she could see a humanoid-blur standing inside the circle. Something tugged at her hair but she ignored it. She gripped the armrest of the bench, knuckles white. Her eyes watered as she tried not to blink, not to let Grace out of her sight for a moment.

Over the hammering of her heart, blending with its drumbeat, she could hear strange music made by no instrument she could identify. Lilting voices accompanied the tune and Harper drifted into a trance. She stood without thinking, taking a step towards Grace.

The music flew to a frenzy, taking her heartrate with it, so fast the blood rush left her lightheaded. It crashed through her as it crescendoed, pipes and fiddles racing faster and faster.

"Harper?"

Grace's voice broke through Harper's reverie. As soon as her sister laid a hand on her shoulder, the music stopped. She blinked slowly and looked around. Her foot was hovering over the circle.

"What's going on, Gray?" Harper staggered back, clutching Grace's hand.

"We've reached an agreement. The faeries aren't the ones taking people but they know who is. If I can arrange a dog-walkers' association who will clean up the park then the faeries will chase away the kidnapper."

"What about the people who already vanished?" Harper asked.

Grace shook her head. "They went through the circle. Apparently, the question is not *if* they'll come back, but *when*. The faeries have agreed to send back one person, a month from tonight, if the park is kept cleaner. That's the best they can do, they won't risk angering the Piper."

"The Piper?" Harper queried.

"The one taking people."

"Which person comes back?" Saqib asked as he came up behind them.

The trees rustled again and the distant sounds of traffic intruded. The spell had lifted.

"Our choice." Grace's expression was grim. "Who gets their life back and who stays lost for a hundred years."

"Sometimes it really doesn't feel like winning," Harper said.

Grace hugged her around the shoulders. "It really doesn't."

THE TAILOR AND THE ACIC'M

For my husband, Chris, who was an ACICM and is now an MCICIM.
A Valentine's Day gift, written in texts from the tram on my daily commute.

"So how did your family get into the coven business?" Harper asked. Grace was on a night shift and the nightmares had been particularly aggressive. She'd been wandering a little aimlessly when she'd noticed the light under AJ's door and heard the clack of his keyboard. Admittedly, she'd invited herself in, but he'd deigned to let her stay.

"It's been part of our bloodline for generations." AJ shrugged without looking up from his monitor. "Ever since the reign of Queen Mary I."

"How did they survive the witch hunts?" Harper pressed. "At a time like that, how did they even get into magic in the first place?"

"Thanks to our faery-stepmother."

"Stepmother? Don't you mean godmother?"

AJ turned from his computer with an exasperated sigh. "Remember when I said you could sit in here if you were *quiet*?"

"You said nothing about *not* being able to sit in here if I asked questions," Harper countered.

"If I tell you the story, will you shut up?" AJ asked. "I'd like to get some work done tonight."

Harper lay down on his bed, head propped up in her hands as she looked at him with an eager expression.

"Fine," AJ grumbled. "It all starts with my great-great-great-something grandfather. He was the youngest son of seven, forced to make his own way in the world. Having a talent for working with needle and thread, an exceptional eye for design and a gift for smooth-talking, he soon became well known as a tailor to the nobility of York and the surrounding area ..."

As well as excelling in business, these talents led him to be admired by many women. After several years of playing the field, he eventually chose as his bride the beautiful daughter of the Flemish merchant who supplied most of his cloth, thus gaining a lucrative lifetime discount. Over time, they were joined by seven beautiful children.

One day, a young woman came to the tailor's store. She was a new customer, or at least the tailor's wife thought she was. Her appearance was utterly forgettable: medium height, mousey brown hair, and a plain but well-made dress. She appeared neither rich nor poor. She turned no heads and her presence almost went unnoticed. She wore no jewellery save a long, gold chain, the adornment of which was hidden beneath her bodice.

Despite her disparity with their usual clientele, the tailor's wife greeted the woman and enquired as to the nature of her visit.

"I have come to buy a dress," the woman mumbled somewhat vaguely, her eyes downcast.

"Did you have a style in mind?" the tailor's wife prompted. "Is the dress for yourself?"

"No." The woman glanced around the store and the tailor's wife followed her gaze to the children playing by the hearth. "It's for a little girl, a friend of my daughter's."

It was an unusual request, to buy clothes for someone else's child, but the tailor's wife was not about to turn away business and she had a soft spot for children.

"How old is this child?" the tailor's wife asked.

There was silence as the woman regarded the children, her unfocussed eyes giving the impression she was lost in a daydream. The youngest child, a pretty girl with curly, blonde hair, sat playing with the tailor's box of pins. Before the tailor's wife could repeat her question, the little girl caught her finger, a small drop of blood welling up.

As she opened her mouth to cry, the strange woman knelt beside her, raised the offending digit to her lips, and tenderly kissed it better. The girl froze mid-wail, looking up into the lady's eyes in bewilderment. Then she giggled.

"The child for whom I am buying the dress is the same age as this little one," the woman answered the previous question as if nothing had happened. "She has not arrived yet, but she will come soon to be a companion to my child. Make a dress this little one loves and I am certain my daughter's companion will love it also. I will return in one week."

With that, she dropped a leather purse onto the counter, turned, and left without another word.

The tailor's wife rushed over to her child, grasping the girl's hand to check her injury. Yet, if she had not seen the blood with her own eyes, she would have doubted the pinprick ever existed.

The tailor came in from the back room where he'd been sewing and looked fondly upon his wife and children. When he noticed the purse upon the counter, he opened it and peered in.

"Don't …" his wife started to say, but the tailor had already seen the glint of gold coins.

"We have a new commission," his wife explained. "However, it would be prudent to refuse it."

And she told him all that happened, concluding with, "I am certain she is one of the Fair Folk. Tilda's finger could not heal so fast naturally."

"Nonsense," the tailor rebuked. "A pinprick is but a minor matter. I get them constantly. You said there was nothing particularly striking about the woman. We would be foolish to turn away such a generous payment. Even if this woman is a faery as you suspect, it would be unwise to cross her."

The tailor began at once to sew a dress for a little girl, using his own daughter as the manikin to size and style it.

But all day, his mind kept returning to the gold. You see, while during the day the tailor was an astute businessman and dutiful father, at night his soul was consumed by that foul pair of demons: alcohol and gambling.

The tailor stole out of his house late that night, careful not to wake his sleeping wife and children. He made his way through the dark streets of York with an ease born of long repetition, until he reached a dingy little pub on the far side of the River Ouse.

It was a less than savoury place. Most of the patrons sat in solitude, hoods pulled over their faces, heads bowed low over their drinks. Some few sat in small groups but there was none of the cheer one might expect from friends out carousing. Instead, they scowled at each other and at any who dared come near.

The tailor made his way through the smoke-filled common room, his own hood pulled up as far as it would go. With a slight nod to the barman, he went through a door near the back and ascended to the second level.

Here, the hostile silence was broken by the flap of cards, the rattle of dice, and the clink of coins. Everyone looked up as the tailor entered, predatory eyes glittering from the dark depths of their hoods. He drew the bag of gold from his pocket and opened it, showing the contents to the room. No one blinked. Hunger festered in the stale air. Then the games slowly resumed.

The tailor joined first this group then that, a mug of ale in one hand, the other carefully counting out his ever-dwindling gold.

As the veil of night withdrew, one by one the other gamblers slipped away. The tailor was about to leave when a strong hand gripped him by the arm.

The bouncer who detained him thrust a slip of paper into the tailor's hand, then walked away.

5 pounds owed to the house.

The tailor paled, sure he had enough gold to cover his debts. He clutched at the little purse as though it might magically provide a lifeline but it remained resolutely and mockingly empty.

The tailor walked home in a daze, desperately trying to find some explanation his wife might accept. He reached his shop just as dawn broke.

Standing outside was a …

The tailor gasped and stumbled back. He stared up in fear, then blinked and shook his head. In his drunken state he could have sworn it was a hulking creature with eyes of liquid metal, the likes of which should never be seen outside of Hell.

As the sun peered past the houses, the shadows receded and the tailor breathed a sigh of relief, cursing his overactive imagination and the godless brewers of ale. The shock cleared some of the alcoholic daze and he found himself staring up at an ordinary man.

The stranger was an unassuming gentleman in elegantly fitted attire. His high-peaked hat sported a turquoise feather, his cloak was cut short in the new, Spanish fashion, and the pattern of his doublet was exquisitely stitched. The tailor scrambled to his feet and half-tumbled into a shallow bow.

"Can I help you?" the tailor asked, attempting by polite speech to cover the offense of his stale breath.

"I have a statement of account." The stranger pulled a scroll from his pocket. It was neatly bound with a silver ribbon, which he untied with delicate fingers, rewound into a neat spiral, and placed back in his pocket. He released the end of the scroll, pinching the upper corners as it unravelled, the end rolling across the floor until it bumped up against the tailor's foot.

"I beg your pardon?" A frown creased the tailor's brow as he stared at the miniscule writing.

"May I be permitted entry to your establishment? We have much to discuss." The stranger gave a small bow as he gestured towards the shop door.

"Of course," the tailor replied, unsure if his mind was reeling from the stranger or the start of a very nasty hangover. They entered the shop together.

There, standing by the fire, was the tailor's wife, hands on her hips, foot tapping on the floor. As soon as they entered, she lay into her husband, either not seeing or not caring about the stranger.

"Where is it? Where is the gold that lady paid for the child's dress? Where is the money you were paid by Lord Sowerby for his wife's gown? Do you know what your children ate this morning? Nothing! And after you promised them meat two days running."

The younger children sat at her feet in tears but the older children continued with their chores. They had seen this argument too many times to be distracted by the spectacle. The stranger made a note on his scroll but no one was watching. If they were, they may well have wondered where, in such a smart outfit, he managed to keep ink for his quill.

As the argument continued, he sat in the corner, apparently forgotten, and made notes. Every now and then he paused to make a calculation, sigh, and shake his head.

"I'm afraid your credit is quite used up," he interrupted. "You must pay what is owed immediately, lest further action be taken. It is quite a sum, I'm afraid. Shall we discuss method of payment?"

The tailor's wife sank to the floor, all colour draining from her face. "I always knew this day would come," she muttered, her hand pressed to her pounding heart. "You're off to debtors' prison and then what will happen to us?"

The tailor gave the debt collector the same stony stare he had given his wife. "On whose authority do you come here, demanding money from me?"

"Please don't misunderstand." The stranger removed his glasses, rubbing them absentmindedly on his jacket. "I would never be called in to collect something so paltry as human money. No, I have been retained on an altogether more serious charge. My client was satisfied with seven-day payment terms and a partial settlement, but after the results of your credit score, I have to insist upon payment immediately."

The tailor stared at him blankly. The man sighed again with a roll of his eyes. "In short, you owe my client fulfilment of your promise to her, or something of equivalent value."

"What promise? Who is this client of yours?" the tailor demanded.

There was a quiet cough behind him and he turned to see a young lady standing in the doorway.

"We're closed," he snapped but his wife jumped up and hurried over to the newcomer.

"This is the lady who purchased the little girl's dress yesterday," she explained.

"It will be ready for the end of the week." The tailor barely glanced at his customer.

"The debt is due now," the collector repeated. "As I was saying, payment terms are now net, due to the amount of debt accrued."

The tailor stared at him blankly. A soft voice spoke up from behind. "Do you not remember me?"

The tailor looked closely at the woman and shook his head. "I was not in the store yesterday when you came by …" he started to explain but he stuttered to a halt as she looked up. Her eyes were brilliant amethyst, faceted like the finest gemstone and equally hard.

"Fifteen years ago last night, you made me a promise." The woman spoke calmly while the tailor, caught in her gaze, reddened and sweated. "You swore I would be your wife and have your children. In return, I gave you myself. I paid my end of the bargain, it is time you paid yours."

The tailor swallowed nervously, finally able to look away. His eyes sought his wife, but she pursed her lips and turned her head, the slight wobble to her chin the only sign of her distress.

"I would like to discuss payment," the lady said.

"Do you want these children or will you require fresh ones?" the collector asked.

"I was going to take the littlest and accept partial payment, but …" The woman strolled through the assorted children, touching a head here or a hand there, eyeing them as one might eye vegetables for purchase. She nodded decisively. "It would not be right to leave the others. Yes, these will do just fine."

"Please." The tailor's wife fell to her knees at the lady's feet and clutched her skirt. "Please don't take my children from me because of the promise of a foolish man."

The lady turned her gaze upon the wife who answered her stare with an undaunted challenge in her own eyes.

"I believe a spouse is also due," the collector said, peering through his document. "A true payment would first entail disposing of his current spouse however I think it would be a poor deal at current exchange rates."

"He owes me a spouse," the lady said, eyes locked with the tailor's wife. "I would be willing to accept his."

The collector made some calculations then nodded. "This would be adequate." The flash of his teal and silver eyes sliced through the heavy air.

The lady turned and curtsied to the gentleman.

"Thank you, acic'm," she said. "Your services are greatly appreciated." When she stood, she took the hand of the tailor's ex-wife and the youngest daughter and led them to the door. "Our pact is fulfilled."

As the last child filed out of the store, the tailor found himself able to move again. He took an angry step towards the door but was pulled up short by the words of the acic'm.

"Now, as to the rest of your debts …"

Over the next week, the tailor's life became living hell. Unable to appreciate what he had until he lost it, he wandered in depressing sobriety. He would hear his wife's voice in the street or catch a glimpse of his lost children, but by the time he reached the spot where they stood, they had vanished.

A week later there was a knock at the door. A tall gentleman in a bailiff's hat stood outside. "I've come to collect, five pounds owing."

The tailor fell to the floor in a dead faint.

When he awoke, his only view was the ceiling of debtors' prison and the cold, teal and silver eyes of the acic'm.

Having finished his story, AJ turned back to his computer. He typed so fast that his fingers blurred to Harper's tired vision.

"You're descended from one of those kids?" Harper prodded.

With a huff, AJ swivelled his chair to face her again. "Harper. I'm trying to work."

"Look, we met because your relatives wanted to kill me. The least you can do is explain to me where your witchcraft comes from. It might …" She bit her lip and studied her nails as she threaded them through the end of her braid. "It might help me work out where my magic comes from."

"The least I could do was not actually kill you," AJ countered. "And on top of that, I helped you learn enough to trap the Ouse, something I was not supposed to do, and I've been doing everyone's IT work."

Harper sighed and stared up at him with eager puppy eyes. "Please, AJ. I'll do your next two cooking shifts."

He paused, weighing it clinically. "Fine."

Harper resisted the urge to smirk. Anything that let AJ hide in his bedroom for longer was a good bribe.

"I'm descended from the third and seventh children. There are those in our family who do have faery blood, but most of us are pure human, like you are. Blood is important in magic, but it's not the only binding tie. Love is stronger than blood, and the tailor's ex-wife and the faery lady came to love each other very much, and they both loved all eight children as though they'd birthed them. Family transcends blood. So my family inherited magic. Over the years, we've intermarried with other witch families or even humans with latent abilities when the need to diversify outweighed the need to draw in new magic."

"If you know other witch families, do you think someone in your coven might be able to work out where I came from?" Harper clutched AJ's blanket to her chest as hope sparked and fizzed.

"Maybe, with DNA testing, if you have any markers in common with any of us. We've only kept those kind of records for a few years. We could check for the name 'Ashbury' if you're sure that's your real name."

"It is." Harper wasn't sure how she knew any more than she remembered learning to play the violin or being taught to read. Yet she was absolutely certain as to her name. It was a part of her no one had ever been able to take away.

"I'll ask my cousin to look into it. Might take a while since we're definitely not supposed to be helping you."

"Thanks, AJ." Harper hopped up and hugged him tight. He squirmed but gave her a quick pat on the back.

When she let him go, he turned back to his computer. "Quietly? Please?"

"Sure thing." With a smile and a lightness of spirit she'd been missing for a while, Harper flopped back onto AJ's bed, grabbed the book she'd brought in with her, and read quietly until she fell asleep.

Easy as 1, 2, 3

Great Peter tolled three. The bell's sonorous voice echoed through the cathedral, lonely and portentous. As the call faded, another voice sang in key with the bell. It was breathy and distant, the vast emptiness catching and spinning it, its origin concealed.

"A Godly man's work is never done,
Only the truth rolls off his tongue.
Of pious deeds, this is one."

Harper could make out faint words, but she didn't recognise the ghostly tune. The first victim had been found without a tongue. The murderer must be close. Sticking to the shadows, she slunk through the cathedral, searching for the source of the song.

"A Godly man's work is never through,
To hear the Word each day anew.
Of pious deeds, this is two."

The second victim's ears had been sliced off. Harper had a sickening feeling she knew where this was going. She had feared some new spirit had taken up the Ouse's cause and started another Hiding, but the corpses lacked the signature runes Saqib found on the Ouse's victims.

When the Guard requested information from the church following signs of a new ghost heard singing a medieval Christian counting song, the archbishop asked Harper to investigate. To the Guard, he had given the official doctrine of the Church: we do not believe in ghosts. Research in the archives and some archaeological finds mentioned in the local paper led Harper and Grace here. Back to the cathedral at the ungodly hour of three in the morning.

"A Godly man's work provides the key,
Through fast and thirst, to eternity.
Of pious deeds, this is three."

The third victim's stomach had been ripped open, intestines strewn across the floor.

Altogether there had been ten members of the cathedral congregation found dead in the last two weeks, all under different circumstances. Harper tried not to listen as the song continued. She didn't need to know their sins. They hadn't deserved to die.

Harper flitted from pillar to pillar, her mottled charcoal-grey clothing blending with the darkness. As she got closer to the whispery song, other faint noises disturbed the stillness and a remembrance of incense hung in the air.

Click, swish. Swish, click.

A door stood ajar ahead of her, candlelight guttering in the draft.

Harper stood in the shadow of the door and peered through the thin gap between the hinges. Beyond, a spiralling stairwell dropped away. Blind corners and hidden recesses. A perfect trap. Harper loosened her machete in its sheath.

She turned towards movement, glimpsed out of the corner of her eye. In the opposite transept, a Grace-shaped shadow raised a hand to point to another stairwell down. Harper gestured 'yes,' and the shadow slipped away.

Taking a deep breath, Harper headed down the winding stairs.

The air grew cold as she descended. The flickering candlelight made the shadows leap and dance across the smooth walls. When she reached the bottom, Harper paused and looked around. Faint echoes of the song ricocheted off stone.

"A Godly man's work should be a sign,
Just as is the bread and wine,
Of pious deeds, this is nine."

Harper tiptoed further into the undercroft of the cathedral. A faint blue glow spilled out from the door to the ancient crypt.

Grace reached the door at the same time Harper did. With a swift volley of hand signals, they confirmed their plan and entered the crypt together.

Click, swish. Swish, click.

A monk paced at the end of the row of archbishops' tombs. He wore a long, tatty robe with pearlescent rosary beads hanging from his belt. Despite the rustle of his robes and the clack of the beads, his sandals made no sound against the stone floor as he circled the end tomb. The Ouse's second victim, the cathedral's own deacon, had lain there the last time she had been down in the crypt.

A body lay swathed in white linen. Where its hands met atop its chest, viscous crimson glooped and stained. As she drew nearer, the Scent of iron cut through the incense and seared Harper's nostrils just as her Sight burnt her eyes. Splayed around the corpse's head, ten dismembered fingers formed a halo. They gleamed gold to her Sight, each knuckle and nail outlined and distinct. She bit her lip hard, battling down her churning stomach.

The monk continued its song.

"A Godly man's work will help reach heaven,
Good works, then Grace, then sins forgiven,
Of pious deeds, this is 'leven."

Although it appeared to have no corporeal form, it was able to move digits over the dead woman's head, adjusting them to perfect symmetry. The monk gleamed in the darkness, its body a mass of tiny blue lights. Blood dripped from its fingers to stain the hem of its robe.

Harper and Grace snuck closer, using the tombs for cover. When they reached the end of the crypt, Harper waited until the ghostly apparition had passed before standing. She thrust out her machete level with its neck.

"Stop and declare yourself," she demanded. The song ceased. The spirit turned, its eyes aglow with bright, blue fire. There was anger and vengeance in its ruthless gaze and Harper took a step back in spite of herself. "Who are you?"

Swish, click. The monk took a step towards her.

"Come no further." Harper took another wary step back. The corner of a tomb stabbed her pelvis, drawing a sharp intake of breath.

Swish, click.

"Harper…"

Ice plunged down her spine as the apparition spoke her name.

"Confess your sins, child, and you may yet see God's light."

Swish, click.

The monk reached out. It passed straight through the thrust of her blade. A hand cold as the grave encompassed her own and Harper's weapon fell from numb fingers. Her heart hammered in her chest, but she couldn't move. With a slow smile, the monk resumed its song.

"A Godly man's work, the world to tell,
God conquered death, the devil fell.
Of pious deeds, this is twelve."

"Step away from her." Grace's voice was as cold as the monk's and her dark eyes showed no mercy. She had circled around to approach from the side and her crossbow was level with the spirit's temple. Its head turned slowly, and it stared at her for a long moment.

"Grace by nature, true to name. No quarrel with you, have we."

"Well, I have a quarrel with you." Grace nodded pointedly at the crossbow bolt tipped with glass, reflecting the monk's gleaming blue light. "Release her."

The monk took a single step back and folded its hands into long sleeves. "You cannot stop us. We will uphold the work of our brethren."

"What are you?" Harper rubbed her hands together. Her heart knocked painfully against bone, her arms leaden, feet frozen to the cold, stone ground. The tomb behind her ground against the base of her spine.

The monk's voice was hollow and faint, but its eyes never stopped burning. "We are the memory of the community who first followed God's Word in this place. They taught those who dwelt here to follow Him and demanded penance from those who fell from God's Grace. Our brethren went to Him a millennium ago and we slept. Now we awaken, as the devil seeks to wrest God's temple from mortal hands. We will cleanse this community and deliver the unrighteous to their damnation. 'Stipendia enim peccati, mors.'"

"'For God did not send his Son into the world to condemn the world, but to save the world through him,'" Grace riposted with a different quote. "You are a memory of a sad and bygone era. Your salvation-by-deeds has no place in the modern church who know humanity is saved through Grace alone. You who kill God's children are not of God. You are of the devil. Still, I give you one last chance. Depart this place, never to return."

"We do God's work. This community will remember His teachings and be born anew. The ungodly must repent and do penance. Why do you, a true believer, protect this unbeliever?"

"Because she is my sister and I love her." Grace stepped between Harper and the spirit, her crossbow never wavering. "And because she, too, is a child of God. I will not let you take another life. This is your last chance, memory. Begone, else I shall prove you are not of God."

"No such proof exists." There was a hiss in the monk's breathy voice. "We are nothing but of God."

It lunged forward, clawed hands grasping for Harper. She tried to clutch at Grace's back, to move away, but her fingers and feet wouldn't respond. Her vision swam, stone clawing up her spine as she dropped. Her knees cracked against the ground.

As soon as the apparition moved, Grace fired. When her quarrel hit the blue light, it exploded. The water within the delicate bolt cascaded through the monk. Its eyes dimmed as it looked down.

"What have you done?"

"I banish you, unholy remnant of a past best left forgotten." Grace walked around the slowly dissolving spirit.

"You cannot. We cannot leave God's work unfinished."

"Your work is of the devil," Grace repeated. "If you needed any further proof then consider this: if your work was of God's will as you claim, why would Holy Water harm you?"

"No … It cannot be."

"It is."

Grace fired a second bolt into the apparition. It, too, exploded as it hit the blue light and the spirit faded with a last plaintive cry. A rosary clattered to the floor, lying in the puddle of Holy Water. When the monk vanished, the blood rushed back into Harper's limbs.

"I knew those Holy Water-filled bolts would come in handy." Grace cheerfully patted her crossbow. She reached down a hand and tugged Harper to her feet. "This will be an interesting one for Saqib to investigate."

"Thank you." Harper flung her arms around Grace who gave her an awkward one-armed hug in return.

"I would never let anything harm you." Grace frowned, then added, "If I let you die, then whose clothes would I steal when my mother insists I wear something garish?"

"Colourful," Harper corrected as she stood back to examine the puddle. "Do you think it's gone for good?"

Grace knelt and picked up the beads. She studied them for a moment then tucked them into her pocket. "I think so, but I'll give these to Godfather just in case. He can perform a cleansing then return them to their original owner. They probably were buried with one of the deceased they found at that old gravesite last month. That's probably what stirred up this 'memory.'"

Harper stepped over to the tomb where the apparition's last victim lay. Tears pricked her eyes as she placed her hand against the woman's pale cheek. Even with the demon gone, the heaviness lingered in her heart. "I'm sorry we couldn't save you. Whatever supposed sin you were killed for, I hope you are with God now."

Grace placed a hand on Harper's shoulder. "I'm sure she is. We'll leave her here. Godfather will ensure she gets a fitting burial."

Harper nodded, placing her hand over Grace's. "Let's go wake up the archbishop. He's had to bury far too many people of late."

Unspoken, but gouging deep pits in Harper's stomach, was the guilt. If she hadn't stopped the Hiding, would this woman have died?

The Monks' Counting Song

A Godly man's work is never done,
Only the truth rolls off his tongue.
Of pious deeds, this is one.

A Godly man's work is never through,
To hear the Word each day anew.
Of pious deeds, this is two.

A Godly man's work provides the key,
Through fast and thirst, to eternity.
Of pious deeds, this is three.

A Godly man's work should God adore,
He falls to his knees upon the floor.
Of pious deeds, this is four.

A Godly man's work should always strive,
From the Saints' sweet words to derive.
Of pious deeds, this is five.

A Godly man's work is to affix,
Always in his mind, the crucifix.
Of pious deeds, this is six.

A Godly man's work, is never hidden,
To confess his sins, he must be driven.
Of pious deeds, this is seven.

A Godly man's work is to donate,
To tithe his wealth, God's wrath to sate,
Of pious deeds, this is eight.

A Godly man's work should be a sign,
Just as is the bread and wine,
Of pious deeds, this is nine.

A Godly man's work is to repent
Of pride and sin and say amen.
Of pious deeds, this is ten.

A Godly man's work will help reach heaven,
Good works, then Grace, then sins forgiven,
Of pious deeds, this is 'leven.

A Godly man's work, the world to tell,
God conquered death, the devil fell.
Of pious deeds, this is twelve.

Look What the Cat Dragged In

Pigeon? Gross. Rat? Definitely not. Mouse? Maybe. What? No. No mouse. Fish. Fish sounds good.

A cat paused at the end of an alley, sniffed cautiously, then trotted across the deserted market square. There were no people around so close to sunrise. He walked with poise and purpose, too elegant to be a street cat. With pristine, snow-white fur and a bejewelled black collar, this cat was no stray.

Once he reached the other side of the square, Zero slowed to a more leisurely pace. With his master's errand complete, he had a little time to himself. The rising sun promised a glorious day and he paused to bask on the gold-lit yet chilly pavement. After dozing for several minutes, he jumped up again. His time was not infinite, and his master would be displeased if he was late coming home. Still, there was time for breakfast.

Zero made his way down to the bank of the river. He had no idea which river it was or even which town he was in, but it was one he'd visited before and the fishing was good. Humans knew it too—there were several small boats already abroad upstream. Zero ignored them, finding a place where the rock sloped to the river's edge. He crouched down and peered into the water. Flashes of colour darted beneath the surface and he grinned, pink tongue flicking out. *Breakfast.*

As one flash came too close, Zero struck. Sharp claws slashed cold water. But he came up empty-pawed. With only a slight twitch of his tail, Zero settled in to wait again. Another bright fish came up to the surface, but it was too far out. Not realising the danger, the fish came to the surface again, this time nearer to the waiting cat.

Once more, Zero thought, his whole concentration on his prey.

As the fish rose a third time, Zero pounced. His teeth closed on nothing but water. Damp and spitting, he backed up in frustration. He was running out of time. He shouldn't have stopped to sunbathe. After a quick glance at the distant fishermen, Zero decided to risk it.

He dipped his paw into the edge of the river then traced a summoning circle on the rock in front of him. It glowed blue then a fish jumped out the water and into the circle's centre. Zero pounced on it and pulled it out of the circle before it could flop back into the water.

As he enjoyed his breakfast, the circle glowed again. *Yum,* he purred. *More breakfast.* A second fish smacked onto the stone and he pinned it under his paw while he finished the first. A static shiver shimmied under his skin, emanating from his collar. He shook his head in irritation, not ready to go home yet. The fish clogged his throat as he finished it off in a few quick mouthfuls.

The call came again, zinging in his veins, more felt than heard. An inescapable bloodbond. But … fish. He hadn't eaten properly in two days and his grumbling stomach was louder than his master's demand he return home. Who knew when another opportunity for fish would come. *Greedy, selfish cat.* The debate raged only a moment before hunger won.

As Zero got started on his second course, the circle glowed again.

I should erase that. Or … or I could eat more fish. It's water. It will dry soon. Until then, I get fish. I like fish. His master's call was more insistent, tinged with irritation, but wasting lifeforce was against his master's ethos, so, really, he was doing the right thing by eating more.

A third fish, larger than the previous two put together, flopped up onto the shore. Zero's eyes lit up. He pounced on his catch, licking his lips in anticipation. His hunger somewhat abated by his first two catches, Zero flipped the fish aside and stalked after it. As it flapped ineffectually, he pawed at it and it smacked him in the face with its tail. Zero jumped back with a curse, rubbing his bruised nose. He pounced on the fish again and pinned to the ground. It flailed at him with ragged fins, unable to escape. Strange noises issued from its mouth. Zero paused in confusion. Then something hard hit him in the stomach.

This was not normal fish behaviour.

Ears flat against his head, Zero backed away.

The creature before him could hardly be called a fish upon closer examination. Although it had the body of a fish, two knobbly legs sprouted from its midsection and it had frog-like webbed feet. It used its fins to push itself up, standing unsteadily, and turned to stare at Zero. Puffing out its chest, it curled its fin into a fist and shook it at him.

Zero hissed softly, taking a tentative swipe at the creature. It was slow and made no move to retaliate but its shouting grew louder. Zero had no idea what it was saying but he could guess the gist. Keeping his body between the fish-with-legs and the water, Zero advanced upon his prey. With a sudden leap, he bowled it over and closed his teeth over its throat.

It was heavy and almost as big as he was, but also slippery enough to slide across the rock easily. Zero dragged it into the bushes. He hated himself for what he was doing, but his master's wishes were inescapable, and he could no more disobey than he could fly. He scratched irritably at his collar.

Pinning the creature underneath him, Zero tapped the air three times with his paw and a portal of swirling violet and silver appeared. Zero nudged the creature through, then followed.

Time and space folded, scrunched, and unfurled.

He emerged in a massive hall with stone colonnades and a cold flagstone floor upon which the fish-with-legs lay whimpering. Zero turned his head away, an un-catlike prickle of tears in his eyes. He wished he'd never cast the summoning circle. *Greedy cat. Selfish cat.* Heart hurting more with every step, he nudged the creature forward with his nose.

Flicking torchlight illuminated what most visitors to the castle took to be tapestries. Zero knew better. The images lacked corporeal substance—being nothing more than light and shadow woven together—yet their purpose was anything but decorative. The landscapes varied from gently rolling countryside to elegant, gothic cityscapes all exuding a serenity belied by the figures of humans and animals within them writhing in pain, their contorted smiles a mask unable to hide the horror in their eyes. The torchlight likewise cast Zero's shadow, and that of his prey, as grotesque, jerky mimicries twining in and out of the pillars.

At one end of the hall was a raised dais with a single throne and a tall table with a crystal bowl of teal water. One of the throne's arms supported a deep purple cushion. *My place at my master's side.* Zero kept his eyes on the ground, unable to look without pride and revulsion clashing.

He crawled toward the throne, prodding his prey ahead of him. *Prey.* Hunting to eat was natural but this turned his stomach. The fish that had so delighted him earlier now rose in acid chunks to clog his throat. He kept his head down, ears flat and belly low to the floor. Ignoring his master's call was always trouble, but it had been his first solo trip to the outside in weeks. Probably his last for several more. There would be no sunlight. Just cold castle walls and darkness. *I deserve no better. If I'd only come back, I wouldn't be in trouble. And neither would this fish. My fault. Bad cat.*

When Zero reached the bottom step to the dais, a black void sparkling with starlight swirls materialised above the throne. Darkness dripped like rain, streaking into a shadowed, humanoid form. Starlight and void masked the figure's face.

Zir voice was multi-tonal and at the sound of it the tapestry figure's mouths gaped in silent screams. "A gift, Zero? To temper my disappointment? Do I not feed you, Zero? I give you what is best for you, you know this. Too much clouds your judgement and makes you lazy. We have too much work to do for that. Too many people relying on us, do we not?"

Zero bowed and mewed softly. *Greedy cat. Lazy cat. Letting everyone down again.* He glanced across at the fish who cowered on the floor in front of his master. *Especially you. I'm sorry.*

Hiding his regret, Zero trotted up the steps to take his place at the foot of his master's throne and was rewarded with a pat on the head. "Despite my sorrow at your actions, Zero, I am intrigued by the gift. Shall we see where this fine specimen comes from?"

His master descended to stand before the captive creature. Drawing a sharp knife, ze leant over and the fish gave a little cry. Zero closed his eyes, a paw over his face. When he dared crack an eye open again the fish-with-legs was sitting, trembling, on the floor and his master was standing by the basin watching the fish's blood drip from the knife into the water.

Zero joined his master, balancing on the bowl's plinth to peer in curiously. An image formed of a rudimentary settlement on the banks of a river. Other strange fish-creatures walked between wooden huts. A few carried basic tools and weapons, others ushered their young in front of them and some paused in small groups, talking speedily in their garbled, bubbly language. An overwhelming fishy smell rose from the basin and Zero licked his lips again.

"Greedy cat," his master scolded. "Did you not feast enough at the river? Must I teach you a lesson for your betterment yet again? I am a busy soul, yet I must constantly pause my work to teach you."

Zero cringed back, eyes rolled away, ears flat, the tip of his tail twitching. He mewed again, trying to convey his sorrow and plead with his master not to harm his find, not to punish some other sentient soul for Zero's own bad behaviour.

His master chuckled and patted his head. "It was a good summoning circle. I will teach you how to be more specific in the future. Yet something interesting came of your failure. Come, Zero. Let us return our little friend to his village, they will be missing him." Relief and gratitude for his master's leniency flooded Zero and his trembling lessened. *Ze isn't angry. Disappointed, yes. But not angry.*

He mewled his thanks softly—his master rarely decided to let captive gentlesen go once ze had them within zir castle walls.

"Its return shall show us a path to them," his master added and Zero flinched.

Ze picked up the fish-with-legs and brought it over to the bowl. It looked down at its village in silence before looking up into the swirling voidmask. It spoke slowly, its tone pleading. Zero couldn't watch. He bared his teeth, a little chitter escaping until the tip of the blade dug into the base of his tail. He closed his mouth, desperately trying to swallow the burning bile in his throat.

His master lowered the fish into the basin and it swiftly dived to the bottom of the deep water. The image rippled then cleared. The fish-with-legs was surrounded by a group of its fellows, all talking excitedly.

When his master turned away, the image vanished. Ze clicked zir fingers and Zero dropped down to the floor to follow zir out of the hall to whatever lesson awaited.

Girins in the Code

I have a job for us.

Harper shook her head in amusement and texted back.

Come have breakfast with us and tell us properly, AJ.

Half an hour later, the door to the kitchen creaked open and AJ popped a sheepish head around it. The other three were still lounging at the table, in PJs and slippers, enjoying a leisurely cup of tea. Grace took her feet off the spare chair and gestured for AJ to join them.

"You took your sweet time." Saqib pushed a box of cereal across the table.

"I was in the middle of something. You folks wouldn't understand."

"More likely we wouldn't care." Grace plonked her feet in AJ's lap. He gave her a brief glare but said nothing.

"So, what's the job?" Harper asked.

"A friend of mine messaged that someone's been hacking computers all over town. Private businesses, council offices, all sorts. His company are specialists in online security but they can't work out what's going on. Ergo, he called me."

"You're better than a whole company of specialists plus all the other tech support in York?" Grace nudged his leg with her foot, hard enough to sploosh coffee out of the cup he was holding.

AJ tried to hide a smirk behind his mug. "I'm the best. Tim wants me to go work for them permanently, but I always say no."

"Why?" Saqib asked. "It's got to be better money than you make … How exactly do you make money anyway?"

AJ grimaced. "Not interested in working for someone. Regular office hours, accountability, seriousness, having to talk to actual people …"

"Oi, what are we?"

"Irregular people," Harper interrupted. "Can we please get on with it?"

"Yeah, so I had a look into it last night and it's definitely not a regular hack. Whoever did it isn't bypassing security, they're completely ignoring it." When AJ saw their blank looks, he added, "Harper can pick a lock and open the door but Heresy goes straight through the door as if neither it nor the lock existed. Get me?"

"It's supernatural?" Saqib asked. "What are they after?"

"As far as I can tell, nothing." AJ frowned, rubbing his chin. "I think they're doing it for fun. It's as if all the computers woke up one morning and decided Egyptian hieroglyphs would be a neat font."

"So, we're dealing with something from ancient Egypt?" Harper asked.

"That was just an example," AJ continued. "It's been all sorts of … Grace, if you're going to use me as a footstool then stop wiggling … all sorts of different issues. One company found all their finances changed from base ten to base thirteen. This morning, our local councillor's documents opened as video files of cats. Cats who were accurately reading the contents of the documents."

"Are you sure it isn't …?" Harper glanced towards the front of the house where Heresy was guarding the door.

AJ shook his head. "First thing I checked. It wasn't Heresy. I know his footprints as well as I know my own hard drives."

"You caught Heresy. Can you tell what it is this time?"

"No. Whatever it is, it's long gone by the time I'm accessing the computer."

"You haven't left the house, mate," Saqib pointed out.

AJ gave him a withering look. "I don't need to."

"But there might be physical evidence," Saqib protested.

"Or we might catch them in the act if we can predict the next target," Harper said.

"Hence 'a job for us,'" AJ said with an exasperated huff. "Normally you would be surplus, but I have reason to believe there is a physical element to the hacks."

"You know where it's going to be?" Grace asked.

"I have an idea," AJ said. "We should all go. Well, minus the little hacking freak."

"Don't refer to yourself in the third person," Saqib said.

"You know what I meant." AJ kicked Saqib under the table. "I'm outta here. I have stuff to finish up ready for tonight. We know the hacks happen around midnight, so be ready to leave here by twenty-three hundred. Harper, bring the lock picks."

"Yes, sir." Harper gave him a mock salute. AJ pushed Grace's feet off his lap and stalked out, taking his half-eaten breakfast with him.

"Don't forget to bring back the bowl," Harper called after him but the only response she got was the slamming of his door.

"Such a delight when AJ joins us for breakfast," Grace commented as she made herself comfortable again.

"Well, I've got to get ready for work. I'll see you tonight unless something juicy comes up earlier." Saqib stood as well, depositing his bowl in the sink.

"Please don't say 'juicy' in relation to crime scenes," Grace begged. "Some of us are still eating."

"Don't you have work today as well, Gray?" Harper asked with a smirk.

Grace's eyes widened as she checked her watch. "Shoot. Guess I better hurry too. Hey, Saqib, give a girl a lift?"

"No chance," Saqib called back as he scurried out the room. "You'll make me late. Sorry, Grace, gotta run."

Grace hurried out of the kitchen, leaving Harper alone with her tea.

"Guess I'm the only one not working this weekend," she said to her cup.

At exactly eleven that evening, AJ, Harper, and Saqib gathered in the lounge.

"Where's Grace?" AJ looked at his watch for the tenth time. "She's late."

"You forgot the rules." Saqib grinned. While AJ paced, he lounged on the couch, watching with amusement. "Always tell Grace to meet half an hour before you actually want her to be anywhere."

"I have to set up when we get there."

"Don't worry." Saqib flopped onto a pillow, resting his feet on the armrest. "If she doesn't show in a few minutes, we can always go without her."

"Go without whom?" Grace swung around the doorframe to peer down at Saqib.

"Grace, you're supposed to be ready to go." Harper grabbed her sister's hand to pull her out of the room but Grace slipped from her grasp.

"I am ready to go," she protested.

Harper eyed her footwear doubtfully.

"I'm ready to go," Grace repeated.

"Can we please get out of here." AJ grabbed both women by the arm and spun them towards the exit. "Heresy, open the door."

"And where are we all going on such a dark night?" Heresy asked pleasantly from his home in the front door peephole.

"Out," AJ said shortly. "You stay here and watch the house."

The door opened with a deep and sorrowful sigh. AJ kicked it on his way past, dragging Harper and Grace with him. Saqib sat on the couch for a moment then got up with a chuckle and slouched after them. They wouldn't leave without the only person who had a driving licence.

They parked a couple of blocks from the office AJ had identified as the next likely target. The building was dark save for small points of green emergency lighting which gave the structure an eerie glow. AJ settled down with his back to a tree at the edge of the parking lot.

"Keep your eyes open," he warned.

"Thanks for the advice," Grace said, rolling hers. "Keep our eyes open. Never would have thought of that, hey Harp. Because we've never done this before."

"Shush," AJ said. "I'll keep an eye out technologically. You guys are here to stop any physical intruder. Just in case."

"We're your bodyguards," Harper supplied.

"So why am I here?" Saqib asked.

"Fodder." Grace flashed him an evil grin. "C'mon Harp, let's check the exits then find some good ambush point to lie low."

Grace pulled a small crossbow out of the bag as she spoke, fastening a belt of bolts around her waist. Harper drew her machete.

The area around the building was as quiet as was to be expected. Then AJ's hushed voice came through the radio.

"Game on."

Harper watched over AJ's shoulder as he typed, the flashing occult symbols as meaningless to her as the actual code.

"Anything physical?" she asked. "Grace is getting bored."

"They're in the computer system. Now shush."

"In the computer, hmm …"

Harper took a piece of chalk out of her pocket and drew on the back of AJ's laptop.

"What are you …? I don't have time for vandalism, Harper," he muttered, his eyes locked on the streams of code.

Harper placed her hand on the sketch, murmuring a few words quietly to herself. The symbol glowed vibrantly.

"Get ready," she warned, taking a step back. Grace pulled out a pipe and tranquilliser dart then stood behind AJ while Saqib stepped behind a nearby tree.

A small creature burst out the back of the laptop and flopped to the floor, shaking its bulbous head in confusion. It was only about a foot high, with a bald, swollen head and spindly limbs. It rolled up into a ball, knobbly fingers clasped around a swollen stomach as if it was in pain.

"Aww, it's just a small … Ow!" Harper reached over to pat it and pulled back sharply as pointed teeth snapped at her fingers.

The circle glowed again.

"Uh oh," Saqib whispered.

A second goblin-like creature, similar to the first but with straggly hair, plopped out of the summoning circle. It grabbed the first one and dashed under a bush.

"Catch them," Harper shouted at Grace as the circle glowed again and a third creature fell out. The glow didn't fade and soon it was followed by a fourth, fifth and sixth.

"Tie them up," Grace suggested, as her dart thudded into the ground, narrowly missing her target's legs. It gave a great belly laugh and pointed at her mockingly before darting away under another bush. Grace growled.

"With what?" Harper asked. "We should've brought a net. Saqib? You could help."

Saqib shrugged. "You've got things under control."

Grace managed to snipe one of the creatures as it grabbed hold of Harper's leg. It let go with a strange yowling noise and plucked the tranquiliser dart out. A broad tongue licked the point then the creature threw the dart away in disgust.

"Back to the crossbow it is then," Grace muttered. If anything, the creature she hit was more hyper than it was before. They were fast and laughed maniacally as they ran, pausing to grin with gleaming white fangs, always dodging Grace and Harper's attempts to grab them.

Saqib leaned against his tree and announced, “I have a body bag in the car if it would help.”

Both women paused and even AJ looked up from his computer.

“You do?” Grace asked with a worried glance at Harper.

“Of course he … Ow. You little f … Ow. Gray, help me.”

One of the creatures took advantage of Harper’s distraction and climbed swiftly onto her head where it clutched her hair with gleeful malice, its sharpened fingernails digging into her scalp.

Grace managed to grab it by the waist but it clung to Harper, babbling incoherently, changing language with every word.

“Will you hurry up?” Harper begged, kicking out at a second creature which was attempting to tie her boot laces together. “תועבצאה וליאכ יל שיגרמ ילש חומה דותב ולש”

Grace frowned and Harper paused, open mouthed. “?המ יתרמא”

Grace managed to wrench the creature off Harper.

“What are you saying?” she shouted and Harper stared back, wide eyed.

Harper tried again, but though her thoughts were English, a language she didn’t know came out her mouth. “גשומ יל ןיא”

“We should get a linguist on the team,” Saqib mused as he sauntered back, bag over his shoulder. “Here Grace, chuck that thing in here.”

Grace held the creature by the scruff of the neck. It swung helplessly, waving knobbly fists at her. She tossed it into the sack with a snort of derision.

“Don’t you dare let it out,” she warned Saqib.

“This is why I don’t do fieldwork,” AJ muttered to himself before adding louder, “I’m done here. I think I’ve worked out a patch for the system which will stop them hacking it again.”

“You can help us round them up then,” Grace said.

“Nah, I’ll wait in the car.” AJ closed his laptop and left with a casual wave over his shoulder.

“רוזחת הפל עכשיו ומיד, AJ” Harper balled her fists in frustration. *Whatever that little freak did to my brain, please don’t let it be permanent.*

“At least look up how to fix Harper,” Grace called after him and he gave her a backwards thumbs up.

After much stress and multilingual swearing, Harper, Grace and Saqib managed to get all six of the creatures safely bagged. Confined in the bag they stayed relatively quiet, cuddling together and whispering with intermittent giggling.

Harper sat down on the floor with a sigh, “?המ השענ םתיא I don’t want to banish them where I sent the cow-eater. Oh.”

"At least it was only temporary." Grace plopped down next to the sack.

"Thank goodness," Harper added fervently. "So what do we do with them?"

"Send them to the Zookeeper?" Saqib suggested.

"I don't want those things in my house." Grace's harsh tone didn't match the careful pat she gave the bag. "Are you prepared to do the run tonight? I'll come with. I'll even help with the driving."

"You so much as lay one finger on my steering wheel …" Saqib gave her a horrified look then glanced at Harper who was laughing.

"Okay, I fell for it," he admitted, "but I will do the run tonight. You can keep me company, Grace, I know you enjoy a trip to the Zookeeper's. You coming, Harper?"

"Sure …" Harper started but Grace cut her off.

"Nope. You have a big day tomorrow. You need your beauty sleep. And you really, really need it, Harp."

Harper rolled her eyes. "Thanks Mum, I'm sure it'll be fine. I can always nap in the back seat on the way home."

"How long ago was your last date? And you're going to blow it just to visit a freak zoo? You're lucky we ran into Theo at the hospital last week."

"Lucky?" Harper raised an eyebrow at her sister. "For starters, we were there to examine a corpse. Just because that poor woman doesn't appear to have been killed by supernaturals doesn't mean we can be flippant about it."

Grace grimaced, holding up her hands. "Okay, fair. I'm sorry. But it wasn't entirely *un*lucky Theo was getting off shift at the same time we arrived. It wasn't *un*lucky it was getting dark and he had to wait for the night bus so you had time to chat. It wasn't—"

"Grace, it wasn't luck at all," Harper cut in. "Do you really think I don't know you planned that?"

"Well, you aren't his patient anymore and he already knows about your job."

Harper waved a hand at the torn-up grass around them. "He doesn't know about this."

Grace shrugged. "You need a date."

"Can you continue this argument later?" Saqib stepped between them. "I do not want those creatures getting loose and wrecking my car so I'd like to head out as soon as possible, if you please. Harper, are you coming?"

"Count me in." Harper stuck her tongue out at her sister. Beauty sleep indeed.

"Okay, road trip." Saqib rubbed his hands together and grinned. "Let's get these in the boot and see if AJ wants to come too."

"Ten bucks says he doesn't," Grace replied.

"I'll take that and raise you five that he not only comes but lets me use him as a pillow on the way back," Harper countered as the three of them carefully lifted the bag between them.

"Bet you another five he's so wrapped up in his computer he won't notice any of it," Saqib added.

Late the next morning a very tired Saqib went to bed a lot richer than he had been when he woke up twenty-four hours previously.

Whispers in the Dark

We're watching...
watching...
We're waiting...
waiting...

Voices scratched at the shadows and scored cold nails down Harper's spine. They whispered – discordant, overlapping, jarring in the quiet of the archives. She slammed the silver gilt tome shut. The dull thud rebounded between the mahogany shelves of the Fourth Vault. It echoed back and forth until it pattered out. The book heaved beneath her hands and she dug in, all her weight against it. With a last grumbling flutter of pages, the book settled.

She cocked her head to the side.

Silence.

Resting her head on her hands, Harper leant against the book, the ornate cover digging into her elbows. She wasn't used to books having a behaviour issue and reading a book one had to close every few minutes was proving to be a hindrance to her research. The way the book spat out bookmarks was also unhelpful. She wasn't even supposed to have it. Her level of archive access acknowledged such books existed but the church's official stance was that all books containing magic were to be assessed and destroyed. Alfred had smuggled it out of the Ninth Vault for her since the archbishop was conveniently deaf every time she requested he upgrade her clearance.

Silence lingered. No footsteps. No rustle of pages. No woosh of messages in the pneumatic pipes. Most importantly, no voices. All sane archivists were long since safely home, none risking the stricter curfew or the early darkness of December. Only Harper and Alfred remained, and their sanity was certainly debatable. Harper couldn't recall a time Alfred hadn't been in the archives. She was fairly convinced he lived there.

Harper patted her pocket, relieved to hear the crinkle of paper. Without the archbishop's official signature on that slip, she couldn't risk being out after curfew either, the hard Damascus steel strapped to her calf notwithstanding.

With a furtive glance around, just in case, she opened the book and resumed her reading.

A distant susurration disturbed the still air. The pages of the book fluttered, slicing her index finger with their silvered edges. Harper sucked it quickly, before blood could seep into the paper. She scanned the book with her Sight, searching for the answer hidden there. A breeze tickled her ear.

Come.

Too soon. They were getting faster. Or maybe they never really left. She loosened her machete, leather grip solid and real against her palm.

"Who are you?" Her voice was swallowed by the heavy atmosphere, thick with dust and the scent of glue and paper. "What do you want?"

We play.

We eat.

We're coming.

All the hairs on her arms stood on end. Each rapid breath hung in the air. Harper snapped the book closed.

Sssssooooooonnn …

When the last whisper died away, she fastened the book's clasps and padlocked it shut. The back of her neck itched, but she could See nothing around other than unending cases of books. The seemingly empty hall gave no comfort. She knew too well the nooks and crannies, where anything might be hidden, watching.

After returning the book to Alfred in one such alcove, Harper shouldered her satchel with a slight grunt. Her footsteps barely made any noise as she made her way out of the archives. With a quick wave to the nightguard, she left the sanctuary of the cathedral and emerged into the cool night air.

Heavy, grey clouds allowed no hint of starlight or moonlight to breach their stern barrier. Her breathing quickened. Too dark. Too close to the Solstice. Her fingers clenched, nails digging into her palms. A light spray of rain bounced harmlessly off her umbrella, drops shaken loose by her trembling grip. When she reached the bus stop, she forced her feet to a standstill, toes curled in her boots. She wanted to keep going. Keep walking. Run.

Before the Ouse, when the curfew was a guideline, not a law, she might have considered dashing the mile or so home, but not now. Now, she would wait for the night bus. Obey the law. Avoid the Queen's Guard. The itch in her back hadn't faded and she cast a furtive look over her shoulder.

Guard or demon, something was watching.

The light above stuttered, blinking shadows on the ground, twisting, reaching. Harper stepped back, closed umbrella tense in her hand.

White and red lights zoomed by—black cars almost invisible in the dark. Their wheels tossed up dirt and water from the damp street. The sound of tires on wet tarmac was too like the distant voices of the book.

Another car flashed by but this time the light remained, a single white globe hovering in the middle of the road. It bobbed up and down in the wind, unfazed by the increasing rain.

A battered van sped past, wheels creaking in protest. The globe swung violently and shrieked in reply. As the van disappeared into the dark, the light resumed its slow bob but the creaking continued as if it swung from an antique chain.

Harper closed her eyes and adjusted her Sight. When she re-opened her eyes, she beheld the wispy outline of a small figure standing in the centre of the road. Ze glistened softly in the rain, bright eyes glittering. In one hand, ze held a lantern aloft. The other beckoned Harper closer.

Another car roared by, but the creature didn't flinch as the car passed straight through. Ze smiled at Harper and beckoned again. She stood, her umbrella forgotten as she stepped out of the meagre sanctuary offered by the bus shelter.

This time the whispering she heard was more than the sound of the rain.

We're here.

We're behind you.

Harper glanced around but she could see nothing through the pelting rain.

Not there.

Over here.

Behind.

No matter which way she turned, the voices taunted her, always hidden from her Sight. The figure in the road caught her eye and ze gestured again. Harper stepped forward involuntarily.

One step.
Two steps.
Off the kerb.
Three steps.
Car.
Four steps.
Five.
Six.
Lantern.

When Harper reached the dusky figure, ze backed away, never breaking eye contact. The ferocity of the rain drenched Harper. Its chill was no match for the cold trickling through her vertebrae and pressing against her hammering heart.

Seven steps.
Eight.
The voices called.

Just ahead.

Just behind.

Above.

Below.

Nine steps.
Ten.
Brakes screeching.

Water thick with human detritus careened down the gutter and engulfed Harper's shoes.

Eleven steps.
Kerb.

Harper stepped up, her legs moving on autopilot, her mind lost in the dream. Rain plastered her hair to her face and dripped onto her cheeks like forgotten tears.

Almost there.

Be with us.

Don't look back.

Twelve steps.
Thirteen.

Harper stepped onto the water-clogged grass at the edge of the Museum Gardens. High above, trees moaned and swayed.

Fourteen.

Fifteen.

The figure paused, zir lantern the only illumination. Ze twisted zir head this way and that, pointed ears pricked. Words drifted to Harper, hidden in the howl of the wind.

Follow

Fly

Fetch

Fear

The lamp-bearer beckoned again and Harper took another step.

Sixteen steps.

Seventeen.

Eighteen.

Nineteen.

Harper dropped her bag as she walked forward, her belongings spilling out into the pooling mud.

Twenty.

She walked on, not heeding her blurred, dissolving notes, all she had gleaned from the cursed tome.

Twenty-one.

Her foot struck something solid and Harper paused. The light ahead winked out.

We're coming.

We follow.

We wait.

As if in a trance, Harper lifted her foot.

Love us.

Hear us.

Worship us.

Fear us.

Twenty-two steps.

We will love you.

We will keep you.

We will consume you.

Harper paused again, an internal battle waging as her foot hung, heavy and uncertain, caught between one step and the next.

We're waiting.

We're coming.

Harper put her foot down.

Twenty-three steps.

The wind screamed through the trees all but drowning out a triumphant whisper.

We're here.

The words clawed behind Harper's eyes like rusty nails and her Sight blazed.

She took a step back.

And another.

Then another.

Harper ran.

As she dashed past, Harper scooped up her bag, barely paused to snatch up her scattered notes. She reached the bus stop just as the night bus rolled up. She fumbled for her pass, ignoring the driver's questioning look, then collapsed into a seat. It was only then she realised she'd lost a shoe somewhere in the mud. Harper checked through her bag; her notes were ruined. Not a single word remained intact. Maybe it was for the best.

Far behind, one last voice whispered on the dying wind.

Next time, Harper ...

Next time ...

A Deal with the Devil

"Your name has been coming up in a lot of our case files recently, Miss Ashbury." A woman in a grey suit waved an armload of manila folders. Each landed with a clang as she slapped them down on the cold metal table. "A Jane Doe with no eyes. Found in a tree. By you." *Slap.* "A demon possessing the River Ouse. *Supposedly* vanquished. By you." *Slap.* "The monks of Micklegate Priory claim *you* tamed a demon." *Slap.*

"I wouldn't say 'tamed'—" Harper tried to interrupt but the woman bulldozed over her.

"A vengeful spirit at the cathedral. Exorcised. Again, by you." *Slap.*

"Technically, that was a De S—"

"Police report stating you and someone they refer to as a 'forensic supernaturalist' detected and nullified a faery threat." *Slap.*

"Well, Saqib works for—"

"Another exorcism, this time on a little girl." *Slap.* "You have been busy, Miss Ashbury."

"Maybe I would be less busy if you were doing your job." Harper's eyes widened in horror as the reproach passed her lips. That was a Grace thing to say. She shifted on the hard, metal chair, straightening her spine and giving the interrogator a cold stare, trying to summon every shred of De Santos superiority Grace exuded. "I work for the Council of Faiths. When members of our communities go missing, or turn up dead, you're damn right we take an interest."

The woman's jaw clenched, her mouth a thin, chapped line. *How does this work for Grace?* Harper wanted to shrink away from the look that lanced her roiling stomach. She clenched her hands in her lap to hide her whitened knuckles.

"What is your secret?" The woman leant forward, hands braced on the table. Her auburn bun was so tight it stretched her skin across her skull. Wide hazel eyes caught every tremor, every trickle of sweat from the bright lights of the interrogation room. The last time Harper was here, her questioner had been the blandest man she'd ever seen. Nothing to distinguish him. Utterly forgettable. In contrast, the intensity of this woman dried Harper's throat and glued her tongue to the roof of her mouth. This time, the crossed halberds and floating crown stitched over the woman's breast pocket told Harper exactly who was examining her.

Harper stiffened, resisting the urge to push her chair back or rub the prickling hair on the back of her neck. Each time her lungs expanded, they shoved her palpitating heart against her ribs. She took a painfully tight breath. "Secret?"

"How are you detecting these incursions? Why are you getting involved now? How are you able to vanquish these evils, if indeed you are vanquishing them?"

Sometimes I have visions of them. Sometimes I scry for them. Occasionally we hear about them on the dark net. Harper clamped her mouth closed. Her hand rose of its own accord, desperate to probe the tightness around her throat, to slip between flesh and the phantom noose. Scrunching her fist into her skirt, Harper held it firmly in her lap. *What would Grace do?*

"When the Council are notified of a missing member of their communities, we are asked to investigate." Harper was relieved the squeak had left her voice. She sounded almost confident, to her own paranoid ears at least. "As I'm sure you know, my degree is in supernatural history. You probably have the permit I needed to study it right there in that pile of yours. I was raised by the De Santos family and I *know* you have stuff on them in your files. My sister and I have been trained to recognise and destroy supernatural influence. We also work with a scientist who is based right here at the police station, the one you mentioned earlier. He's working on ways to detect magic with his equipment and the police chief often asks him for help. You can see it's all above board and we have all the correct permits and authorisations. There are no secrets. We want York to be safe. Can you say the same?"

The was a sharp hiss of breath as the Guardswoman leant back. She folded her arms over her chest. A thrill of exhilaration ran through Harper. *Does Grace feel like this all the time?*

"Of what *exactly* are you accusing the Queen's Guard, Miss Ashbury?"

"Nothing." Harper lounged back, crossing her legs, letting a slight smile play across her lips. "I'm sure the Queen's Guard want nothing more than to keep York's citizenry safe. I'm sure every report you've shared with the Council has been open and thorough. In fact, while I'm here I can take some files back with me if you want. I know Archbishop Marshall sent a request in yesterday. I'd be happy to act as messenger."

The Guardswoman gave Harper a jagged smile, sharp enough to saw through bone. "I was hoping you'd offer."

Harper blinked, the smile slipping from her face. "You were?"

The woman tapped the pile of documents, a sharp staccato in the echoing interrogation chamber at odds with her saccharine tone. She didn't blink when she spoke, her eyes locked on Harper like a bird of prey watching a mouse. "Of course. You have quite the success rate here. And as you say, we all simply want to keep York safe. We should be working together. You, your foster sister, the scientist in the precinct, even the freelance coder who lives with you. Just as the De Santos family work with us in Canterbury. I am sure neither you nor the Council of Faiths would object to a partnership, in the best interests of York, of course."

Harper cursed herself for walking straight into their trap. *Grace makes having authority look so easy but I screwed it up again. Maybe it* is *a genetic De Santos thing.*

"Of course," she replied through gritted teeth. "We'd be delighted to work with you to make York safer and get to the root of these arcane invasions."

"Excellent. I'm sure it will be a most profitable partnership." The Guardswoman held out her hand, a crocodile smile on her lips, the gleam of a predator in her eyes. Harper shook it, knowing her adversary would take victory in her clammy palm and trembling fingers. "Good day, Miss Ashbury. I look forward to talking to you again soon. Please pick up the documents your archbishop requested from the front desk on your way out."

Even after the woman gathered up her documents and left, Harper didn't relax. She couldn't see the cameras, but they were there. Her stiff walk and tense shoulders gave her away anyway, but she wouldn't give them the satisfaction of seeing her weaken. She made it about three quarters of a mile from the police precinct before she collapsed on the grass at the edge of the cemetery. The ghostwalkers might claim the dead watched the living, but Harper knew better. The dead were only ones who weren't watching her at the moment.

"And Faustus hath bequeathed his soul to Lucifer," she muttered. She tugged her collar down and rubbed her throat. If there was a God, she hoped Ze understood she had no choice.

Soul-Crushing Black and Bubblegummiest Blue

For Sarah Fletcher and PSC Willis.
Without your support and love, Zero would not be the cat he is.

Nightmares knew better than to stalk a dreamwalking cat. Not that they needed to haunt Zero. The wakening was his nightmare: an endless cycle of blood, hunger, and guilt. Inferior nightmares slunk away from a reality they couldn't hope to match. Which made them all the harder to catch. Collecting nightmares grated his nerves raw. Zero was used to his 'normal,' but other people's nightmares had the power to leave him sobbing for nights afterwards, curled up in front of a cold hearth too afraid to seek the comfort of his master's bed. Children's nightmares were the worst. A shiver rippled his fur when he sensed one on the horizon of the dreamscape. The throat-constricting, heart-stopping horror was something that could never be articulated.

Describing it as darkness didn't capture the way searing light burned through to illuminate a dreamer's greatest fear. How it forced them to experience minute, excruciating details which darkness might have kept mercifully hidden. Comparisons to thunderstorms and grey clouds leant the false idea that nightmares were monochrome. They were blood-splatter red, gold-plated knives, electric blue, brassy guns, and yellowed gnashing teeth. Storms were natural and beautiful. If nightmares were natural, Zero would eat his own tail. They certainly weren't beautiful save to a sick and twisted mind. What they were, was Power.

Power the Veil consumed with the recklessness of a starving abhartach greedy for children's blood. It was his duty to collect them so his master might feed them to the Veil and protect England. Zero's mind shied away from other uses for the twisted dreams that his master swore ze'd never do. Magic didn't like liars, so it must be true. Distrusting his master, the only person to love him and care for him, would be like clawing out his own heart. Ze would never unleash a nightmare for revenge or punishment.

His master never punished.

His master taught.

Zero shook off the thoughts and concentrated on stalking the child's nightmare. He had no physical body in the dreamscape, yet his mind provided sensations of crouching and crawling forward with his belly nearly in the non-existent dirt. The closer he got to the rampaging beast of the nightmare, the heavier and colder his heart grew. Imprisoned within the maelstrom was a young boy, a kitten not old enough to have strayed from his parent's side. Zero hissed, metaphysical claws unsheathed.

Terrifying solitude punched him in the chest as he entered the dreaming. All his fur stood on end with the static tension of waiting, of shivering in a corner, of not knowing when sharp pain would come. There was almost safety in the absolute certainty that it would. Whether emotional or physical didn't matter, not in the dreamscape where both could shred a heart.

The lightless room created a terror that looped between Zero and the dreamer. There was no mercy in darkness this time for it wasn't what the darkness hid that frightened them. It was the darkness itself and the promise it held. Lost memories clawed for purchase at the back of his brain, but his mind was too slippery with blood to hold them. The boy flicked the light switch back and forth, back and forth. The tatty lampshade stayed resolutely dark, the socket within it empty. Monsters had taken the bulb.

The bedroom door was locked. It was always locked. The window was locked, too, and sealed shut by paint layered over blood layered over paint, a fresh coat applied after every failed escape attempt. Bleeding fingers were left untreated as a reminder of failure. *You are not smarter than me. You are not stronger than me. You belong to me.* The child scrabbled at the frame. Scabs caught on splinters of wood and metal and ripped free of half-healed skin. No broken glass. Not tonight. He wasn't that desperate yet. Scars on his arms ached as a reminder of times he was.

The nightmare pounced on those fears and memories. Heavy footsteps, slow and inexorable, beat stairs barely shielded by threadbare carpet.

Thud … Thud …

Shadows lengthened and the room expanded and shrunk. Furniture became impossibly high yet the gaps beneath bed and desk were too tiny and claustrophobic to offer hiding places.

Thud … Thud …

The boy grabbed the painted-over window lever, heedless of how the ragged metal bit into his palms and drew a fresh layer of blood.

Thud … Thud …

The handle rattled. A key scraped into a lock. Click. Clack. When the door squealed open a crack, a fishy scent permeated the room and a thin beam of light pierced the darkness.

Zero and the boy sobbed with relief at a glow that seemed brighter than the sun. They squinted, afraid to waste a second of it. The light might not last long.

As the door swung open, a shadow robbed them of the brief relief. Swirling with the aura of a nightmare, the outline of a featureless man loomed over the tiny cat and young child. The boy cowered in the corner, knees drawn up to his chin and hugged tight by trembling too-thin arms.

The man's face was invisible. Zero scrutinised the void where expression should be. Monitoring tiny facial clues was one of his only defences, but the nightmare denied him even that glimmer of hope.

A sharp intake of breath drew Zero's attention back to the boy. No. Not a boy anymore, although still a kitten. Teenager, Zero guessed, although human ages were hard to work out. Maybe he was a little younger than Zero, a few years, no more. The teen's eyes were glazed and he swayed as he stood, as if he were intoxicated. Defiance in his posture sparked cold against the internal anger of his father.

"Can't handle the washing up on your own?" the boy taunted. Zero winced at his rebellious tone, but the dreamer only breathed deeply, his chest swelling in mirror of the anger swelling in his father.

The nightmare's response was the garbled words of a challenged dream. The boy wasn't fully lucid, but some bit of him knew this was a nightmare he needed to fight. Zero twined around his ankles, silently cheering him on.

"I do *everything* in this house," the boy almost shouted at the figure, responding to whatever often repeated argument was playing out.

Repetitive nightmares that fed on a fear for years were excellent batteries. It might even give the boy some short relief, until another nightmare stole in. Still, guilt squirmed in Zero's gut. Nightmares could be healing, if one could beat them, and the dreamer struggled for it so valiantly.

The shadowy man took a step into the room, fist raised, making Zero's decision for him. This evil figure was the epicentre. Remove him, and the nightmare could be contained. Zero pounced, claws out. There was a shout of surprise from the dreamer, then hands closing around Zero to drag him off. The overwhelming fear had a different flavour. Not fear for *me,* but fear for *you* as the boy shields Zero in his arms.

No. Helping you, he told the dreamer, understanding in the dreamscape being more than words. The boy's grip slackened and Zero pounced again. The man tried to throw him off, but cats are stubborn. Zero dug in with claws and teeth, biting down hard as the bitter taste of nightmare choked him.

Thick fingers grasped his fur in response. Hairs were ripped from his body as the father tried to throw him off. Zero hissed, but the pain was nothing compared to home. A fist flew past him as the teenager pummelled the man, too, still attempting to protect him. The dreamer breathed deeply, a crazed look on his face, then he fell back, eyes wide with fear as he gazed at the bloody mashed nose of his jailer.

"I'm sorry. I didn't mean to. I'm a monster. I'm sorry."

As a different kind of terror warped the dream, the shadowy form Zero had pinned writhed and shook off his grasp. Before Zero could pounce again, the father retreated and slammed the door with the reverberating crash of iron bars. The key turned in the lock and the last glimmer of light was extinguished. The boy ran at the door, beat it harder than he'd beaten his captor, but to no avail. He was locked in. In the dark. Again.

The man had gone but the nightmare was still there. It *was* the darkness. Inside the boy's head, gnawing at his darkest secrets and consuming his fears.

Zero twisted between the boy's ankles until he was picked up by rough hands that left him dangling, his back legs unsupported. The teen meant well. He tried to cuddle Zero against his chest, muttering small comforts to calm the shaking kitty. Zero snuggled with him, eyes scrunched closed, until their twin heartbeats slowed. Gradually, the boy eased back into normal sleep aided by the background mutter of a soft, feminine, almost cat-like voice. His embrace faded, and Zero was left alone in the dark.

He had the nightmare under his claws and he lost it. His master would be disappointed. Fear paralysed him without the distraction of comforting the dreamer. Air molecules were too large to fit down his throat. Wait. He didn't need to breathe. Not in the dreamscape. The shock of the realisation shook the fear loose and allowed Zero to function again. This was his domain and he wouldn't let his mind warp it and create flimsy, useless nightmares. Still quaking in anticipation of the lessons he'd need to complete if he woke up empty pawed, Zero continued his pursuit of a powerful nightmare.

After being twice more defeated, the shaking in his soul worsened. He had nothing to show for the night's work. The sensation of tears prickled behind non-existent eyes. Since he couldn't catch a nightmare, his master would expect him to provide the power, insubstantial though his abilities were in comparison. He didn't want to wake up. Ever.

His heart wanted to reach out for a comfort like the maternal voice that had lulled the dreamer to pleasant sleep. But pain would snap him out of the dreamscape if he didn't come willingly. Nowhere was safe. There was nowhere he was wanted, nowhere he could go …

A swirl of colour twinkled over him. Pretty, sparkly speckles like a shattered crystal. Pounce. Zero chased it, darting back and forth through it as lights stained his fur. He dropped into the dream, manifesting a physical form.

Paint rippled like water each time Zero's paws dipped in it as he trotted through the dream. Blue, pink, and purple splodged the landscape, with other colours dotted in between as if someone had shattered pieces off a rainbow and splashed them around in a frenzy. Although abstract, the dream he'd strayed into was vivid. It was smells and feelings, not simply colours or sounds. The puddles each had their own scent and each scent felt so complete it was as if it was the epitome of that thing.

The spiciest pink, flavoured with cinnamon, chilli, and peppercorn, burnt his tongue and made him lick his lips as his stomach growled for more.

The richest purple, softer than his fur, creamy without diminishing the pink's spice, a silken promise that tied his stomach in perplexing knots.

The bubblegummiest blue, cold as ice cream, sour as candy, popping each time he stepped in it. It zinged with friendship that left an ache of longing in Zero's chest.

Zero wasn't even sure where the word 'bubblegum' came from. Something in the dreamer's mind providing him with words for things he didn't know. That was unusual, especially as the dreamer didn't seem aware of his presence and wasn't particularly lucid.

More paint splashed, droplets splittering against his white fur. Woven through the main colours were flashes of rainbow.

The sunshinest yellow tasted of tropical fruits and carried the warmth of an island breeze. It riffled through his fur, while the warmth of the brightest smile soothed his nervous heart.

The sharpest green came with a tang of pickle that the cat shied away from.

The rollercoasteriest red was charged with inaudible screams of excitement and a rush of adrenalin that left Zero dizzy but eager to experience it again.

There was music in the air. It zinged with colours and complex patterns that were unfamiliar save in this dreamer's mind. They made Zero's paw tap and the tip of his tail twitch in time.

Normally, Zero loathed being wet, but the paint in the dreamscape was different to water in the wakening. He enjoyed its touch and its taste. He pranced through the puddles, pounced on reflections, and basked in the lightness of spirit and creative flair of the dreamer.

His master couldn't follow him here. Ze was tied too strongly to the wakening. Despite years of Zero trying to teach his master how to straddle the realms, ze had never been able to set so much as a toe in the dreamscape. Zero had been given many lessons on how to teach better. A tiny voice at the back of his skull wondered why his lessons hurt so much to receive when those he gave were soft. Maybe his master suffered the pain without yowling like a pathetic little cat. Zero wiped a paw against his eye, accidentally smearing his face with lavender paint, to hide the very human tear forming. *Stupid cat. Selfish cat.* He should go before he tainted the beautiful, joyous dream.

"Here, kitty kitty. Here, pretty kitty."

The dreamer was aware of him? Zero twitched, looking all around. The consciousness hadn't changed, wasn't lucid enough to truly know he was there, yet it still wrapped around him. It held him there without forcing. Welcomed him. No. It couldn't. It was too beautiful for a selfish, worthless little cat.

"Stay, pretty kitty?"

Although the sun couldn't be seen, it was bright as a Jamaican beach and glistened off sea blue pools of paint. It had a warmth and comfort that begged to be basked in. Zero couldn't say no to it. He stretched out by a pool of violet that mirrored the magic gleaming in his eyes. A tropical breeze smoothed his fur like a stroking hand. Safe.

A sharp snap of pain stabbed through the dream. The yowl that reverberated might have been Zero's or it might have come from the dreamer. Even in the dream, Zero's tail hung at an unnatural angle. A command vibrated through him with enough force to shatter bones.

COME BACK. It started under his collar and zipped down his spine to crackle like a frayed wire in his broken tail.

No. Zero fought it. It hurt. It hurt so much. Like electrodes plugged directly into his bones. *I want to stay here. I don't want to go back.* The thoughts sickened him. *Selfish cat. What you want doesn't matter. 'I want' gets folk killed.* He wavered on the edge, knowing he had to go but heartbroken to leave. What if he never found this dreamer again?

COME BACK.

Zero mewled in pain. He sunk his claws into the ground, clinging even as he grovelled.

"Don't leave me."

The feelings rather than the words hooked into his heart.

"I don't want to leave you."

The thought turned into a howl as the dreamscape shuddered and his tail dropped limp into a splash of vermillion paint.

COME. BACK.

His master's command was stronger than his own will or the dreamer's. It wrenched Zero back to the wakening, back to the pain. He opened crystal-blue eyes to blood-splattered fur and his tail bent at a sharp ninety degrees.

Through the Looking Glass

Their first Queen's Guard assignment didn't go well, in Harper's opinion. Conversely Derek, the police detective who'd been sent to work with them, seemed pleased with the results. When Harper asked why, he responded, "Because I don't think the family did it. They're always the first suspects, especially when there's no signs of break-in. It's always a relief to me if it wasn't the people closest to the victim. It's rare, sadly. If someone ever offs me, I hope it's not a family member or a friend."

Struggling behind them with a large bag and two tripods he wouldn't let anyone else touch, Saqib interjected, "You're most likely to be killed by Detective Robinson."

Derek stroked his chin thoughtfully. "Yes, ex-partners are usually good suspect material. Maybe I should get him before he can get me. He did poison my tea once, after we broke up—"

"I think I'll walk back." Harper glanced at Saqib and raised her hands in a question when the detective turned his back to unlock the car. "Poison?" she mouthed.

"Gallows humour, common police trait," Saqib said in a low voice. "Common British trait really."

"Nevertheless, I think I'll walk. It's only a little further from here to the cathedral than it would be to walk from the police precinct."

"Suit yourself." Saqib shrugged. "I'll analyse these samples and let you know if I find anything."

"Thanks. See you at dinner?"

"Maybe, depends how long this takes."

"*Definitely*. It's your turn to cook."

Saqib grimaced. "Yeah, um, sure. See you at dinner then."

"Flatmates are usually good suspects too," Derek pointed out, ignoring Saqib's glare.

Leaving her housemate with the chortling police officer, Harper walked back towards the city centre. When their car disappeared around the corner, a black cat slipped through a wrought iron gate to trot along at her side.

"Did you notice anything?" Harper asked it.

The cat's whiskers twitched. "Very good, Harper dear," he said. "You are improving. You have never spotted me so quickly before."

"I'm glad you think I'm getting better." Harper kicked a pebble down the street as she walked with her shoulders slumped, head bowed in defeat. "I couldn't See a damn thing in that house. We said we'd make sure no one got hurt because we stopped the Hiding, but I have no idea what to do. All these missing women recently. We can't help any of them."

"We were trying to help people?" the cat asked in apparent amazement.

"*Heresy*."

He shrugged off the warning tone in Harper's voice. "I do not know about you, but I was looking for inspiration," he purred.

"I am *not* asking what you mean."

"Inspiration like a mirror reflecting a different room."

"I said I'm not … what?" Harper stopped, but Heresy continued on with a spring in his step.

"Clever trick," he continued blithely. "Difficult to pull off. I am curious to know if it was a real place or not."

"Heresy …"

This time Harper's irritation made the cat pause. He hopped onto a nearby wall and watched her with narrowed eyes. "Are you telling me you did not notice? So sad. Poor Harper."

"Why didn't you tell me? I took you along so you could help."

"It was not a threat? Not in the deal? More fun not to? Your choice."

"Sometimes I think Grace is right about you," Harper accused as she started back up the street.

The cat grinned, its teeth bared. "I know she is, Harper dearest. Sometimes you are as deaf as you are blind."

Suddenly the cat jumped, its hair bristling as it arched its back and hissed. Then it leapt down from the wall and dashed away, disappearing around the corner. It departed so quickly that it left behind a blur of black fur which hovered for a moment before gently drifting to the ground. There the small, dark specs came together in a heavy mist before snaking after Harper. When it reached her, the mist curled around her ankle and ascended to drape itself around her neck.

"Wear out your welcome?"

"Maybe." His voice was low and sullen. Harper smiled, despite her helplessness.

"I'm not the only one who doesn't learn. The cats in York are catching onto your sneaky possessions. Legend does say they talk to each other, you know."

"It is not my fault you refuse to buy me a pet," Heresy grumbled.

"You're here to protect me, not to play with kitties. Now shush, we're here. This time, show me what you saw." Harper crouched, using the overgrown hedge as cover to get close enough to peek in the lounge window of the missing woman's house. Her parents had been leaving for the Shabbat service at the synagogue, so the house would be empty.

Heresy slid off her shoulder and drifted through the glass before settling over the catch on the other side. A moment later, he drifted away again and Harper was able to open the unlocked window. Her sneakered feet made no sound as she tiptoed over the plush carpet to a large mirror hanging on the far wall.

She had glanced at it when she came in previously, but nothing in the room gave her an indication as to why the daughter of the house would have run away or been kidnapped. The father described a happy family, a statement borne out by the many smiling photographs displayed in the lounge. He had stood by an upright piano in the corner of the room. His eyes were tight and moist as he explained how Alice spent many hours in this room practicing. The worn keys looked well-loved, and Harper suspected Alice enjoyed playing rather than being forced. Grace had been made to take lessons and had come to love her instrument in spite of rather than because of it.

The piano was the last place anyone had seen Alice. She'd been playing for her mother and her aunt. While her relatives were in the kitchen washing the dishes, the music had stopped abruptly. Alice's mother had run back to the piano, fearful her daughter had fallen, only to find the young woman gone. The windows and door were closed, all portals to the outside world locked. There was no sign of a struggle; Alice's bag lay by the piano where she left it. The seat was still warm.

In addition to the piano, the room contained two comfortable couches and several chairs, ready for large family gatherings, a long coffee table stretched between them. A mirror on the wall reflected light into what would otherwise have been a dark room on the north side of the house. The table was clear, but when they visited earlier, the family had laid out drinks and food as though they entertained honoured guests, not people investigating their daughter's disappearance.

Harper took a closer look at the mirror. Her own puzzled reflection stared back.

"Do not look at it," Heresy hissed from the shadows under the piano.

"How am I supposed to work out what's wrong if I don't?"

"Look from the side, do not look at your own reflection. She will have you if you do."

"She?" Harper took Heresy's advice and stood to the side of the mirror to look at it almost edgeways. It reflected the room, just as it should.

"The mirrorling. They possess reflections as easily as I possess a cat. Look out the corners of your eyes, use your Sight. Look at the piano stool."

It was getting easier to summon the burning sensation which indicated her magic was enhancing her vision. Harper stood at an angle to the mirror. If she stared sideways, her head tilted just so, she could see the reflection of the piano out the corners of her eyes. The patchy seat appeared out of place in an otherwise well-cared-for home.

Harper squinted, fighting the urge to look properly at the reflection. The stool bowed in the middle, as though it had been sat on for so many years it had moulded itself to the shape of the user. Or as though someone sat there still.

As Harper watched, a ghostly outline formed of a young woman in a long dress. Her face was turned away from the mirror, but from the speed her fingers danced across the piano keys, she must be Alice.

"I see her," she breathed. "What's happening, Heresy? Am I seeing what happened in the mirror? Has it recorded it somehow?"

"You are seeing what really is," Heresy replied. "Or rather, what will be."

Harper glanced at the piano stool in the real world. It was plush and plump, not worn or indented at all. She watched the mirror again until the image of the pianist returned. Turning her head slightly, she risked a better look. There were spots of age on the woman's hands, wrinkled and blue-veined. The photos along the credenza were faded and yellowed.

"Heresy, is she *in* the mirror? Why is everything in the reflection older?"

"Time passes differently there. For her it is only a minute and it is only a century."

"How do I get her out?"

"You do not," Heresy hissed. "You accept the girl is lost and you leave it alone. Getting through would be easy. Getting back impossible."

"Can I summon through the mirror? Call Alice back?"

The darkness under the piano bristled. "No. Dangerous. You would get the mirror-Alice, the mirrorling's pet. The real Alice probably no longer exists. Not as what she was. It is done."

"I can't accept that, Heresy." Harper set her jaw stubbornly. "This woman has a life here. She has family who love her. I refuse to accept some mirror spirit can abduct her away and there's nothing we can do. What if it takes someone else?"

"Look right at the edge of the mirror."

Harper did as she was told, flattening herself against the wall and trying to watch the mirror surface in her peripheral vision. She got a fleeting impression of a young woman in a flower dress, sitting at the piano and, very, very faintly, Harper could hear tinkling as if a music box had been left open in another room. Another form appeared to be standing behind the pianist, hands on her shoulders, leaning over, and Harper caught the sound of whispers although she couldn't discern the words. The two people merged as the shadowy form leant further forward, until there was only one Alice again, at once old and young, endlessly playing the piano.

"She will live her life there," Heresy said, his voice muted. "For us it will be minutes or centuries but she will not know the difference."

"And her soul? What happens when she dies? Does the mirror-Alice consume her?"

"Do not ask me," Heresy said nonchalantly. "Someone will find a body, another Jane Doe. If Saqib watches for her, he may be able to match her DNA to Alice, or to her parents, or she may remain a mystery forever. The mirrorling will love and protect her, but she is no longer the person she was. She is happy. Leave her be."

"But her family," Harper protested weakly.

"There is nothing we can do. They might even see her sometimes. They will think it merely imagination, but they will see her."

"What if I smash the mirror?"

"Then you make a million tiny universes and she is trapped in all of them."

Harper sank to the floor, back against the wall. She rubbed her eyes and rested her head on her knees. "There's really nothing we can do? You're not just telling me that?"

"There is always that risk."

"I'm going to the archives." Harper jumped to her feet and brushed away her tears. "I *will* find a way to get her back, no matter what you say. Or Saqib will come up with something. Some scientific wormhole thing or … or something. We will bring her home again."

Heresy chuckled, a dark humourless sound. "No, dear Harper. There is nothing you can do. She is already home."

Christmas in the Shambles

Ancient buildings huddled against the cold, their foreheads pressed together, shoulders hunched and stiff. Snow drifted on the air between them, defying gravity. It settled on tiles and caught in the leaves of garlands strung across the street. Lights twinkled in the gloaming, faery dust dancing with the snow. Cobbles gleamed, slick with black ice, a trap for the unwary. Above the warm glow of shop windows, miniature fir trees burst from the brickwork, their baubles catching and twisting the light. Two stories up, hung between the buildings, wreathes framed eaves and glimpses of the snow-laden sky.

Harper tugged her patchwork coat tighter around her, pulling the collar up to protect against the harsh wind's prying fingers and the Guard's meddling gaze. Two tan-coated men stood by St. Crux church, guarding the entrance to the Shambles. Always they watched, even as night drifted down and winter grasped the streets. It seemed like tempting fate to pass them on the shortest day of the year, but their icy gaze slid over her as though she were nothing but a ghost.

A ghost wouldn't have looked out of place on the warped street. Harper's breath caught in her throat, remembering the ghostwalker who had haunted the street for as long as she'd lived in York. Her eyes burned and a pale outline of a midnight-clad man strode across her field of vision. His tall hat brushed low hanging garlands as his sweeping cloak stirred up flurries of snow. As she stared, he melted away like a snowflake falling on fire leaving a chill in her bones that had nothing to do with frozen air.

"Could I have saved him?" The words slipped from chapped lips, muffled by her scarf. She'd Seen his death and fled, fearing the watchful Guard. Tears pricked her eyes. She *should* have saved him.

Harper paused as she passed a tearoom, the sweet scent of freshly baked cookies wafting on the air. Her stomach gurgled, urged her to enter. Through the panelled window, she could see a stout woman sweeping the floor, ready to close before curfew kicked in. The broom stirred up petals of snow as it flew across the tiles. The woman looked up and crooked a finger at Harper when their eyes met. A longing filled Harper, for the comfort of hot tea and melting treats. The broom kept sweeping, twisting away from gnarled fingers to dance on its own. Harper blinked and looked again. The woman was still sweeping, her eyes focussed on the floor.

With a shrug, Harper moved on. She had her suspicions about the proprietor of the tearoom and her colourful granddaughter, but she'd never Seen anything untoward. Just hints, like the broom, like kettles without plugs, like tattoos she swore moved. She glanced down the street towards St. Crux, the Guardsmen out of sight around the corner. They guarded the Shambles more to make it appear like there was something supernatural there than because they believed there was. It was good for the tourist trade to make it look real. Harper glanced down the street to the paper shop, her smile hidden behind her scarf. Hiding in plain sight.

For once, the paper shop was not her destination. Nor the tearoom, nor the alchemy shop, nor even the Christmas store. She ducked under a curving eave to peer in frosty windows at an elegant green five-string violin. The warm scent of sugar hung in the air as someone exited the fudge stop down the way, but Harper only had eyes for the violin. The twisting vines painted on its emerald body were not dissimilar to the white roses and leaves she'd painted on her own instrument back home, but the shape of the electric violin was nothing like the acoustic's familiar curves. She traced the glass with its hourglass outline and sweeping anchor-esque base.

Strains of music glimmered through the snow, bright against the darkening sky, welcoming the Solstice. The notes thrummed in Harper's ears, a plaintive vibrato capturing the voice of the wind. When voices joined the soaring song, she looked up. Behind her, down the alley, in the Shambles market, a choir had drawn a small cluster of late shoppers. A violinist accompanied their carolling, long blue hair fluttering in the breeze. Elegant fingers danced on the strings, violet flames sparking to her Sight. Voices faded as the strings seemed to wrap themselves around her heart, tight and sharp. Eyes dark as the depths of a river reflected twinkling starlight. He winked at Harper. She stumbled back, her head cracking against the window frame.

"Lovely, isn't it?" A voice commented over her shoulder. The music storekeeper stood with her shoulder resting against the doorframe watching the carollers. "One of my favourite things about Christmas, but then, it would be, wouldn't it? Are you window shopping or coming in? We're about to close." Her eyes flitted down the street then back to Harper. "Got to be locked up tight before the last sun, even though I sleep here and don't have to travel."

"I'm … er … I'm after some sheet music." Harper tore her eyes away from the violinist. "How … how much is the electric?" She gestured to the five-string as she entered the store.

The shopkeeper smiled, taking in Harper's patchwork coat and tatty satchel in unspoken dismissal. *More than you can afford.* "Two thousand and a bargain at that."

Harper gulped and nodded. "It's worth it." She turned away from the violin with a small sigh. Two thousand. Plus the amp. Plus the bow. Closer to three thousand than two all in. Grace would kill her.

"I need to get the violin music for *Crystalise* please. I'm playing it for the concert at the cathedral, slower than the original of course, and I … um … lost mine." In the mud. And blood. To swiping paws and sinister cackles. Harper buried the memory. The shopkeeper tutted but fetched the requested music. As soon as Harper paid, she was ushered out the door and the lock snicked closed behind her.

"Beautiful." The choir had disbanded, heading home before the sun dipped below the horizon, but the blue-haired violinist remained. He, too, was staring at the electric five-string in the window. His own violin was tucked safely under his arm, its wood stained algae green.

"So was your playing," Harper offered awkwardly.

The man flashed her a grin but there was nothing warm in his dark eyes. "You killed my sister."

The world went fuzzy when he spoke. Harper shook her head to clear her ears of ringing. "Pardon?"

"I said, I'd kill for this instrument." His eyes bored into her as the hair on the back of her neck prickled and she shivered. Then he smiled again, his easy, relaxed stance belying his words.

"It is gorgeous," Harper agreed. She rubbed her ear, a persistent heat in the depths of the canal making her feverish. "Do you play professionally?"

His lips parted around his teeth like water breaking around rocks. "You could say that. I … teach. Do you play?"

"Not as well as you. Just for fun mostly, although I had lessons as a teenager, I …" Harper trailed off. *I already knew how to play and I don't remember who taught me but sometimes, sometimes I can hear them playing in my dreams.*

"Music in dreams is a sign of a creative soul." His mouth stopped moving but she could still hear his voice. *"Killers can be creative too."*

Harper's brow creased. Had she spoken aloud? Had he? Every part of her ached with fever, her brain foggy and sodden. "I'm sorry. Did you say something? I … didn't quite catch …"

Long, cold fingers brushed her cheek, leaving trails of icy tears in their wake. *"If you want to learn, I will teach you, Seer of York."* His lips retained their soft smile, never moving as his breath mingled with hers. *"You will play the most beautiful music. No human can compare to what I can teach you. You will play and you will sacrifice. Your fingers will bleed, worn down to bone. Your feet will crack and tear in the eternal dance. Your lips will chafe away, your tongue turn to lead. Your heart will be consumed and your soul shall become a requiem."*

His lips brushed hers and stole her breath. Ice blossomed over her lungs. The taste of mildew soured her tongue. Her eyes and ears burned with fever. Harper scrunched her eyes closed then opened them wide, sure it must be a vision.

The violinist had disappeared. All that remained was a high A keening on the wind. It followed her as she hurried past the Guard, heading for the bus stop. As she left the Shambles, a husky voice whispered in her ear, "*We will meet again, Seer. Come to me when you need to learn. I will wait.*"

Cats Don't Play Fetch

"Five."

A long-haired, extremely fluffy white cat lay sleeping by the last warmth of the kitchen fire. A pointed ear pricked at the interruption of the harmonic voice but he didn't awaken.

"Four."

The distant voice flooded the room, its potency unmuted by the closed doors. The cat lazed open one blue eye.

"Three."

His nose twitched and he closed his eye again, curling up in a small ball.

"Two."

Although he appeared asleep, the cat's fur bristled.

"One."

The tip of his tail flicked back and forth.

"Zero."

With a distinctly put-out expression, the cat uncurled and stretched, his claws scratching the flagstone in old ruts from a thousand wakenings at this spot.

There was a moment of silence as he yawned then the voice called out again.

"*Zero.*"

An accompanying jolt travelled through his collar, down his spine, and along his tail. The cat leapt to his feet and dashed to the door. On hind legs, he pawed at the handle until the door clicked open, then he slipped out into the cold, stone corridor. He slunk through dark halls until he saw light spilling out of a crack under an ornate cherrywood door. As he nosed the door open, quiet chanting drifted out.

After cautiously peering around, the cat tiptoed in, keeping close to the circular wall as he skulked around the room. A hare, a stoat, a butterfly, a raven, and a wolf were peering up at a tall, bubbling cauldron. None of them glanced at their new companion as he silently joined the end of the line-up and sat as if he'd been there all along.

Behind the cauldron, shadows and dust coalesced into a glowing ball of black light. A waterfall of darkness cascaded down the hovering sphere to form floating, voluminous robes. An androgynous white mask coalesced in front of the light, the surface cracked with a web of black ornamentation around its eyes and high cheekbones. Its lips were dark as death and the voids in its eyes could consume souls. It was never a good sign when his master wore that mask.

"Zero."

Zir voice was a cacophony of many people speaking at once. All of them were disappointed. The cat's ears twitched, his eyes locked on a speck of dust as it floated across the floor.

"I will not abide lateness."

Zero lay on his belly and mewled at his master. If he acted contrite maybe he would be forgiven. The creature next to him—a large, brown hare—placed a long foot on Zero's back. The pressure on his back ground his chest against the stone floor. She could break his spine if she pushed a little harder. It wouldn't be the first time master had asked One to teach Zero obedience, wouldn't be the first broken bones Zero had caused himself. *Selfish, stupid cat. Why can't I do as I'm told?*

"Thank you, One, but lessons will not be necessary today," his master said quietly.

The hare removed her foot. Zero sat up, slit eyes promising retribution against One later. Dust clung to his pure, white fur and he resisted the urge to groom. *My master will be displeased if I move out of line.*

A bowl appeared on the floor in front of Zero. He affected a blasé demeanour until the scent of blood struck him and his eyes narrowed further. His lips curled and a small hiss escaped. *Shh. Master doesn't like mouthy, disobedient little cats.*

"Since you decided you would rather sleep than remain ready for my commands, you may have first taste of my latest experiment, Zero."

Zero wrinkled his nose in disgust. He had absolutely no desire to drink unknown blood. *It doesn't smell human. I know human blood. Her blood made me.* In his dreams, he had tasted a nameless girl's tears and smelled her salt and magic.

"Are you hesitating, Zero?" The words were cold as gravestones touched by Jack Frost. They held the same promise too.

Zero shook his head. Shuddering, tears welling in the corners of his eyes, he dipped a paw into the dark liquid and licked a drop.

It burned like he'd swallowed acid again. It stripped flesh and exposed nerves. His tongue, his throat, his stomach, his whole body right to the tip of his fur, every part of him wanted to scream like a witch on a pyre.

Human tears fell from cat's eyes and dripped into the bowl of blood. Zero scowled as he tried to shake the remnants of the disgusting liquid from his paw but it clung to his pads and stained them a deep pink.

"Thank you, Zero. You may go," his master said. "Please be here in twenty-four hours for your second dose."

At the dismissal, Zero limped from the room, avoiding putting his weight on the bloody paw which still felt as though it rested in a pot of scalding hot water. None of the other animals looked at him except One, who glared as her paw twitched toward the bowl. *Jealous? She can have it. I … no … she's right. It's an honour to be the strongest, to share the most with our master, to be trusted by zir. It hurts, but zir magic helps people. She doesn't want to help people. It has to be me.*

As he slunk back through the labyrinthine passages of his master's keep, Zero looked for a warm place to curl up and lick his wounds. The fireside no longer appealed to him. *If only the castle had real sunlight.* For a moment he had a fleeting image of green grass, bright sunshine, and a girl's laughter on the wind. Like a dream, it vanished and left only an impression of light, no matter how hard he tried to remember.

As Zero passed yet another endless passage, he thought he caught movement out the corner of his eye. He pivoted, hissing, back arched as he scanned the darkness. Empty. Just because he could no longer see anything didn't mean there was nothing there. A chill of unease crept through him. *Something is definitely there. The castle doesn't feel right. It knows.*

From victim to hunter in the blink of an eye, Zero crouched, ready to spring. His master may command every creature's fear and respect but away from zir watchful gaze, Zero refused to be intimidated by the other denizens of the fortress. *Even One. I was here first, after all. She's made of my blood, not the other way around.*

Again, a flicker of movement, further down the corridor this time. Zero stalked it, leaving a trail of bloody footprints in his wake. The apparition led him deeper into his master's lair, seemingly knowing its way through the ever-changing corridors and staircases. It always stayed just far enough ahead that Zero couldn't tell who it was yet it remained within sight. Zero glared, he didn't like being mocked.

The apparition led him deep underground. Air hung damp and stale around him, sticking his fur to his back. Ahead, a door creaked opened and drenched the corridor with the light. A fresh breeze whipped past him. Zero leapt back against a wall and screwed his eyes closed against the brilliance. When he opened them again, an apparition stood in the doorway, silhouetted against a sun setting over a city Zero didn't recognise. The figure crouched down and held out an open hand.

"Here, kitty, kitty, kitty."

Zero backed up with a hiss.

"Here, kitty," the apparition repeated. It had a voice like his master, as if many spoke at once, but the pitch was predominantly feminine. It brought a strange sense of déjà vu. He took a step forward. Then another. Then a third. And another, until he was able to stretch and delicately sniff the hand held out to him. The figure was only a silhouette, a creature of black, white, and greys.

As soon as he was close, the hand reached over his head. Zero ducked, flat against the floor, ears back, but it simply rested its hand on his head. It smoothed his fur as it stroked him. Zero purred softly then stopped himself. *I'm not their pet.*

Zero swiped at the hand with his claws. The figure yanked its hand back with a shriek. Dying light caught its face in a golden glow. He pulled back with a loud hiss as he beheld the blank, white mask his master favoured for creating new familiars to sell.

The figure followed as Zero retreated, back arched, fur all on end. It was not his master. It lacked the indescribable power of zir presence, but it looked and moved like zir. Only the voice was wrong.

Corners of the black mouth turned upwards in a grotesque smile as the apparition extended its hand again. "Here, kitty, kitty."

Zero skittered back, his claws out, ready.

The sun had almost disappeared below the horizon. The figure placed a gloved hand over its mask. As it lowered its hand, its face was revealed.

With a yowl, he turned and fled, leaving behind a trail of bloody footprints and a scattering of fine, white hair.

The apparition wiped one footprint with its finger before lifting the bloody digit to its mouth. Black lips became red as blood stained them and a dark tongue greedily licked the last drops away. Then the figure walked into the sunset and the door swung closed behind it.

Zero didn't stop running until he reached his master's private chamber. He frantically scratched at the wooden door until it opened. Then he ran in and hid under the bed. He lay there trembling for many hours until his master returned to zir room. His real master. Ze hung zir cloak up and laid zir mask on the bedside table. Then ze coaxed Zero from under the bed and picked up the shaking cat.

"What did you see, Zero?" his master asked as ze ran zir nails through Zero's fur.

Death. Your death … and hers.

ACKNOWLEDGEMENTS

My deepest thanks to my family, in the UK, the USA, and wherever else they may be. Love is stronger than blood. It doesn't matter how a family is forged if they're always there for each other, and my family are beyond any question or doubt.

Especially thanks to my husband, Chris, who has read all my stories and heard me tell hundreds more. Your honest critique and praise mean the world. I trust your honesty and I *almost* believe you when you say something's good.

To my parents, who are much better booksellers than I am, for your endless support and passion. Thanks also to my sister, Chloe. Your enthusiasm gives me joy.

This collection started life as a series of character development exercises, and many were drafted before I started either *The Hiding* or *The Somnia.* My characters have also developed through the opportunity to chat to friends' characters in the weekly Twitter 'Meet My Characters Monday' (#MMCM). Thank you to all who participate, and in particular members of Team Tea and Books.

Extra thanks to Sarah Fletcher and P.S.C. Willis who know Zero as well as I do. Our crossover fiction gave him life and let me explore many facets of his personality and powers. I had to add a story to this collection because he refused to return to a world that didn't have Reece and Ash in it.

To those who beta read all or some of these stories – Danai Christopoulou, Katya Hernández, Taylor Grothe, Jessica Mitacek, Amanda Casile, Rae Wilde, and Tanya Pell – I appreciate all your feedback and encouragement.

Similarly, thank you to Mire Marke and Henry for their sensitivity reading of relevant stories and to Rabbi Tanya and Reverend Bruce Thompson for their assistance with the Hebrew in Girins in the Code.

Thanks to Heather and Steve of Brigids Gate for taking on more Seer of York stories and for editing, to Elizabeth Leggett for her amazing cover art, and to Stephanie Ellis for proofreading and formatting.

Last, but always first in my heart, my beautiful, mischievous Sprite. You are an inspiration and a delight.

ABOUT THE AUTHOR

Alethea (she/ze) writes various forms of SFF, with a particular love for science-fantasy, dark fantasy, dystopias, and folklore. Many of her works take place at the intersection between technology and magic. She enjoys writing stories with subtle political and philosophical messages, but primarily wants her stories to be great tales with characters readers will love. She also has soft spots for found family, hopeless romances, and non-human characters. Her short stories can be found in a variety of publications, and links for these are on her website.

Alethea lives in Manchester, UK with her husband, little Sprite, a cacophony of stringed instruments, and more tea than she can drink in a lifetime.

Bonus content for The Seer of York seriescan be found on her website: https://aletheaIyons.wixsite.com/stories/seerofyork

Social media: https://linktr.ee/alethearlyons

ABOUT THE AUTHOR

ABOUT THE ARTIST

Elizabeth Leggett is a Hugo award-winning illustrator whose work focuses on soulful, human moments-in-time that combine ambiguous interpretation and curiosity with realism.

Much to her mother's dismay, she viewed her mother's white washed walls as perfectly good canvasses so she believes it is safe to say that she has been an artist her whole life! Her first published work was in the Halifax County Arts Council poetry and illustration collection. If she remembers correctly, she was not yet in double digits yet, but she might be wrong about that. Her first paying gig was painting other students' tennis shoes in high school.

In 2012, she ended a long fallow period by creating a full seventy-eight card tarot in a single year. From there, she transitioned into freelance illustration. Her clients represent a broad range of outlets, from multiple Hugo award winning Lightspeed Magazine to multiple Lambda Literary winner, Lethe Press. She was honored to be chosen to art direct both Women Destroy Fantasy and Queers Destroy Science Fiction, both under the Lightspeed banner.

Elizabeth, her husband, and their typically atypical cats, live in New Mexico. She suggests if you ever visit the state, look up. The skies are absolutely spectacular!

ABOUT THE ARTIST

CONTENT WARNINGS

General:

Blood (minor), violence, weapons, religion, mental illness.

Story Specific Additional Content Warnings:

1. *The Cleansing* – None
2. *Never Alone Again* – Child possession, person burnt by a match on purpose
3. *What's Eating the Cows* – None
4. *The Púca in the Priory* – None
5. *Going Around in Circles* – Kidnap
6. *The Tailor and the Acic'm* – Alcohol, gambling, divorce
7. *Easy as 1, 2, 3* – Mutilated corpse (none graphic)
8. *The Monks' Counting Song* — None
9. *Look What the Cat Dragged In* – Threat of harm to an animal
10. *Girins in the Code* – None
11. *Whispers in the Dark* – None
12. *A Deal with the Devil* – Interrogation, verbal only
13. *Soul-Crushing Black and Bubblegummiest Blue* – Harm to an animal, threat to a child
14. *Through the Looking Glass* – None
15. *Christmas in the Shambles* – None
16. *Cats Don't Play Fetch* – Harm to an animal

More From Brigids Gate Press

THE HIDING

By Alethea Lyons

Arcane archivist Harper has always been plagued by dreams of grotesque creatures and bloody deaths. When she bumps into a ghostwalker in the Shambles and has a visceral experience of his execution, she knows it's a foretelling. Yet fear of the Queen's Guard stops her speaking out. When her vision indeed comes true, the unusual markings on the ghostwalker's corpse, combined with his neatly excised vocal cords, send a ripple of terror through York.

The witch hunt is on. As the body count rises, Harper knows her magic is the only way to find the killer – if she can avoid being hanged as a witch. To protect both human and supernatural, Harper walks the thin line between their worlds. She and her demonhunter foster sister form a multi-faith team with a forensic scientist, a spirit Harper accidentally summoned, and a techno-witch, to catch the killer before more people die.

The Wolf and the Favour

By Catherine McCarthy

Ten-year-old Hannah has Down syndrome and oodles of courage, but should she trust the alluring tree creature who smells of Mamma's perfume or the blue-eyed wolf who warns her not to enter the woods under any circumstance?

The Wolf and the Favour is a tale of love, trust, and courage. A tale that champions the neurodivergent voice and proves the true power of a person's strength lies within themselves.

A Man in Winter

by Katie Marie

‘

A mesmerizing psychological mystery from an author who brings a refreshing new voice to horror. This is a quick read, but one that keeps the reader thoroughly intrigued and entertained from beginning to end.’

—Catherine Cavendish, author of *In Darkness, Shadows Breathe* and *Dark Observation* (coming in September 2022)

Arthur, whose life was devastated by the brutal murder of his wife, must come to terms with his diagnosis of dementia. He moves into a new home at a retirement community, and shortly after, has his life turned upside down again when his wife’s ghost visits him and sends him on a quest to find her killer so her spirit can move on. With his family and his doctor concerned that his dementia is advancing, will he be able to solve the murder before his independence is permanently restricted?

A Man in Winter examines the horrors of isolation, dementia, loss, and the ghosts that come back to haunt us.

Melinda West: Monster Gunslinger

By KC Grifant

KC Grifant comes out guns blazing with *Melinda West: Monster Gunslinger*—a devious action-packed adventure set in a very weird version of the Old West. Fast, furious, and a hell of a lot of fun!"—Jonathan Maberry, NY Times bestselling author of *Son of the Poison Rose* and *Relentless*

In an Old West overrun by monsters, a stoic gunslinger must embark on a dangerous quest to save her friends and stop a supernatural war.

Sharpshooter Melinda West, 29, has encountered more than her share of supernatural creatures after a monster infection killed her mother. Now, Melinda and her charismatic partner, Lance, offer their exterminating services to desperate towns, fighting everything from giant flying scorpions to psychic bugs. But when they accidentally release a demon, they must track a dangerous outlaw across treacherous lands and battle a menagerie of creatures—all before an army of soul-devouring monsters descend on Earth.

Supernatural meets *Bonnie and Clyde* in a re-imagined Old West full of diverse characters, desolate landscapes, and fast-paced adventure.

Visit our website at: www.brigidsgatepress.com

Printed in the USA
CPSIA information can be obtained
at www.ICGtesting.com
CBHW031913270824
13785CB00004B/41

9 781963 355055